"Phire."

Maverick whispered her name the moment she leaned up and offered him her lips. At that moment, he could no more not give her what they both wanted than he could stop breathing.

"Tonight has to be goodbye," she whispered when he brought his lips closer to hers.

Like hell it would be. There was no way he would allow her father to force her into marrying anyone.

When she stuck out her tongue to lick his lips, his guts clenched and he leaned in to capture her mouth with his. He heard the low moan from deep within her throat.

Their kiss intensified. Somehow he managed to ease off the sofa with her still cradled in his arms and their lips remaining locked. He broke off the kiss and whispered, "I want you, Phire."

"I want you, too..."

* * *

The Outlaw's Claim by Brenda Jackson is part of the Westmoreland Legacy: The Outlaws series.

Selected praise for
New York Times* and *USA TODAY
bestselling author Brenda Jackson

"Brenda Jackson writes romance that sizzles and characters you fall in love with."

—*New York Times* and *USA TODAY* bestselling author Lori Foster

"Jackson's trademark ability to weave multiple characters and side stories together makes shocking truths all the more exciting."

—*Publishers Weekly*

"There is no getting away from the sex appeal and charm of Jackson's Westmoreland family."

—*RT Book Reviews* on *Feeling the Heat*

"What is it with these Westmoreland men? Each is sexier and more charming than the one before.... Hot, sexy, smart and romantic, this story has it all."

—*RT Book Reviews* on *The Proposal*

"Jackson has a talent for creating the sexiest men and pairing them off against feisty females. This story has everything a hot romance should have."

—*RT Book Reviews* on *Hot Westmoreland Nights*

"Is there anything more irresistible than a man so in love with a woman that he's willing to give her what she believes is her heart's desire? The Westmoreland clan will claim even more fans with this entry."

—*RT Book Reviews* on *What a Westmoreland Wants*

BRENDA JACKSON

THE OUTLAW'S CLAIM

Recycling programs for this product may not exist in your area.

ISBN-13: 978-1-335-58144-0

The Outlaw's Claim

For questions and comments about the quality of this book, please contact us at CustomerService@Harlequin.com.

Harlequin Enterprises ULC
22 Adelaide St. West, 41st Floor
Toronto, Ontario M5H 4E3, Canada
www.Harlequin.com

Printed in U.S.A.

Brenda Jackson is a *New York Times* bestselling author of more than one hundred romance titles. Brenda lives in Jacksonville, Florida, and divides her time between family, writing and traveling. Email Brenda at authorbrendajackson@gmail.com or visit her on her website at brendajackson.net.

Books by Brenda Jackson

Harlequin Desire

The Westmoreland Legacy

The Rancher Returns
His Secret Son
An Honorable Seduction
His to Claim
Duty or Desire

Westmoreland Legacy: The Outlaws

The Wife He Needs
The Marriage He Demands
What He Wants for Christmas
What Happens on Vacation...
The Outlaw's Claim

Visit her Author Profile page at Harlequin.com, or brendajackson.net, for more titles.

You can also find Brenda Jackson on Facebook, along with other Harlequin Desire authors, at Facebook.com/harlequindesireauthors!

To the man who will always and forever
be the wind beneath my wings and the
love of my life—Gerald Jackson Sr.

In memory of my childhood friend and soror,
Lynda Ravnell. Losing you this year was hard,
and I will forever appreciate the memories.
Rest in peace.

Love endures long and is patient and kind...it takes no account of the evil done to it [it pays no attention to a suffered wrong].

—*1 Corinthians* 13:4–5

One

"I now pronounce you husband and wife. You may kiss your bride."

Maverick Outlaw grinned broadly as he watched his brother Jess pull his new wife, the former Paige Novak, into his arms, as if determined to kiss the lips right off her face. None of the onlookers seemed surprised at such a strong display of passion. Not even their father, Bart.

It had shocked the hell out of some when Bartram Outlaw had shown up for the wedding. It really should not have, since it was one of Bart's sons getting married. However, the Outlaw brothers would be the first to admit that their father was ornery as hell and pigheaded to a fault. There were other words that could describe him, but since none of them were nice, Maverick decided not to think about them today.

Maverick was just glad their old man was here and trying to be friendly and sociable. Maybe that was helped along by the beautiful woman at his side, Claudia Dermotte. She was as friendly, sociable and outgoing as they came.

A few hours later, after all the wedding photos had been taken and the wedding dinner had been served and eaten, Jess and Paige escaped to change into their traveling clothes. They would be leaving to begin their month-long honeymoon, beginning in Dubai.

Maverick swore he'd never seen Jess so happy. There was no doubt in Maverick's mind that although marriage seemed to agree with some people, he was not one of them. He liked his life just the way it was, and he enjoyed being a bachelor. His goal was to remain that way for quite a while. Maybe even forever, since he didn't have to worry about continuing the Outlaw line. His married brothers seemed to be doing a good job of it.

"I noticed you kept your eyes on the old man today like the rest of us."

Maverick glanced over at his brother Sloan and nodded. "I don't know why we even bothered when he's with Claudia. Dad never acts like an ass when he's with her."

"True. That goes to show he can be a decent human being when he wants."

Maverick nodded again, knowing that was true. He wished he could say their father's bark was worse than his bite, but *that* wasn't true. Bart Outlaw was known to take a huge chunk out of a person's ass whenever he was inclined to do so.

Maverick took a sip of his champagne and glanced over at their father. Claudia's hand was firmly in Bart's as she moved toward the newlyweds, who had just reappeared. When they reached Jess and Paige, of course, it was Claudia who made the first move and gave the couple goodbye hugs. Maverick then watched his father give Jess and Paige hugs as well. If he hadn't seen it with his own eyes, he would not have believed it. When did Bart ever hug anyone other than Claudia and their sister, Charm?

"I'd be damned," Sloan said, obviously seeing the exchange as well. "Although he looked stiff as hell doing it, I can't believe the old man actually hugged them."

"I honestly think that stunt he pulled with Cash and Brianna scared the shit out of him," Maverick said, remembering how their father had tried to break up the couple. "He finally realized how close he came to losing one of his sons when Cash was ready to disown the old man."

"I agree with you there," Sloan said. "Maybe that's why he didn't have anything to say when I announced I was marrying Leslie."

Maverick had four brothers, and all were here and accounted for. He also had one sister. He knew some people found it amazing that all six Outlaw siblings were as close as they were, considering each of them had a different mother. Bart had been married to five of the women, and when the divorces became final, his attorneys made sure he was given custody of his five sons. Maverick, at thirty-two, was the youngest son.

Garth, at forty, was the oldest, and he and his wife, Regan, were the proud parents of a seven-month-old son name Garrison. Regan's father had been the corporate pilot for his family's company for over forty years. When he retired, Regan had taken over. Just as Garth had taken over as CEO of their family's multimillion-dollar business, Outlaw Freight Lines, when Bart had retired. Or more specifically, when the company's board threatened to oust Bart if he didn't step down.

Jessup—or Jess, as he preferred to be called—was thirty-eight and became the politician in the family when he went to Washington four years ago as a senator from Alaska. Everyone was happy for him and Paige, who was an actress in Hollywood and sister to their cousin Dillon Westmoreland's wife. Paige had turned twenty-nine today and wanted to get married on her birthday.

Cashen, who preferred being called Cash, was Bart's third-oldest son and at thirty-six was married to Brianna. They were the proud parents of two-year-old twin boys. Cash and his family made their home in Wyoming on a ranch he'd inherited from his mother.

Sloan was brother number four and had gotten married five months ago. He and his wife, Leslie, maintained dual residences in Wasilla and Fairbanks, Alaska. Sloan had had no problem informing the family—the day of his wedding, mind you—that he intended to have his wife pregnant by Christmas. Since that was next month, Maverick could just imagine how the couple spent most of their free time.

Last, but not least, there was his sister, twenty-seven-year-old Charm. She was the youngest of Bart's children, and being the only girl, she was definitely the apple of their father's eye. To this day, Charm's mother, Claudia, was the only woman Bart had ever loved and the one he couldn't handle. And…she'd been the only mother of his children Bart hadn't married, but not for lack of trying.

Hell, their father was still trying. Maverick and his siblings always got a kick out of seeing Bart court Claudia. They figured the reason she hadn't married Bart after all this time was because she needed some sort of affirmation that he had changed his manipulative ways. If that was true, then there would never be a marriage because Maverick and his brothers couldn't see his father turning over a new leaf any time soon, or ever. Just like a leopard couldn't change his spots, they doubted their father could change the ingrained nature of his character.

Sloan walked off, and Maverick was alone again. At least for the time being. There was no way he could ever be totally alone among his Westmoreland cousins. There were too many of them. Besides that, the wedding and the reception had been held in a section of Denver the locals referred to as Westmoreland Country.

Dillon, the oldest of the Denver-based Westmorelands, had built this mega building and named it Westmoreland House. The building, which could hold over three hundred people easily, was meant to be used for special occasions, events and family get-togethers.

Hearing oohs and aahs, he glanced over to where several relatives were admiring his cousin Bane's three-month-old babies. It was the second set of triplets for Bane and his wife, Crystal, and all six kids were a perfect combination of the two of them, though they all had their father's hazel eyes.

Maverick's cell phone vibrated. He had turned off the ringer during the wedding ceremony and now wondered who would be calling him. Most of his female acquaintances only had the number to his burner phone. Anyone he considered important was here, attending his brother's wedding.

Except for Phire.

He felt a slow roll in his stomach after pulling out his phone and seeing it was her, Sapphire Bordella, the woman who'd once been his friend with benefits.

He and Phire had met in Paris three years ago, when he'd been on a business trip. They had been attracted to each other immediately. He had quickly discovered she was someone he could talk to and enjoyed spending time with—both in and out of the bedroom. They were friends who understood each other, and at the time neither had been looking for anything permanent. One thing they had in common—they both had domineering fathers. Maverick knew how to handle his, but Phire had yet to learn how to handle hers. He was convinced the man was as much of a manipulator as Bart. Possibly even more so.

A year ago, Phire had decided it was time for her

to pursue a serious romantic relationship. By mutual agreement they had ended their FWB relationship. However, they had maintained their close friendship and would often call each other to see how things were going. Lately, he'd noticed her calls had become infrequent. He had assumed she'd met someone and things had gotten serious, and he'd been delegated as a part of her past.

"Phire?"

"Yes, it's me."

Maverick heard the strain in her voice. "Is everything alright?"

"No."

That single word stoked his ire at whatever was bothering her. The one thing Phire would never admit to was not being okay. He walked to an area in Westmoreland House where he could hold a private conversation. When he entered an empty room, he realized it was the huge playroom Dillon had added to the design of the building so the youngsters in the family could have a place to enjoy themselves. This room looked like an indoor playground.

"What's wrong, Phire?" he asked, closing the door behind him.

There was hesitation before she said, "I know we're not together anymore, but I need to see you, Maverick."

He heard the urgency in her voice and glanced at his watch. "I'm at my brother's wedding in Denver, but I can be in Paris in—"

"I'm not in Paris—I'm in Texas."

"You're home?"

"I told you this ranch hasn't been my home in years, Maverick."

Yes, she had told him that a number of times. "Alright. I have my plane. Just give me time to refuel and I'm coming to Texas."

"I hate for you to leave the wedding."

"The reception is about to end, and Jess and Paige will be leaving for their honeymoon in a little bit, anyway."

"If you're sure it won't inconvenience you."

A part of him knew Phire could never inconvenience him. "It's no problem. I can fly into Austin's airport and—"

"No, I prefer meeting you someplace else."

"Where, then?"

"Dallas. I can leave here for Dallas in a few hours."

"And I'll meet you there. I'll make all the arrangements and text them to you."

"Okay, and thanks, Maverick."

"Don't mention it. I'll see you soon."

After he clicked off the phone, he checked his watch as he left the room. He hoped to have all his questions answered as to what was bothering Phire in a few hours.

"And just where do you think you're going, young lady?"

Phire didn't bother to glance up from tossing items into her overnight bag. The last thing her father needed to know was that she had plans to meet Maverick. The best thing she'd done over the last three years was to keep Maverick's identity shielded from her father.

When he had ordered her home from Paris a couple of days ago, all he'd said was that she should come home immediately. Once she had arrived at the ranch, it didn't take long to find out why she'd been summoned. He had selected the man he wanted her to marry.

Phire's mother had passed away when she was twelve. Less than a year later, her father, Simon Bordella—an attorney turned rancher—sent her to live with his older sister in Paris. He hadn't even sent for her to come home during the holidays or summers. If it hadn't been for her aunt, Phire honestly don't know what she would have done. Lois Priestly had been a godsend for her.

As Phire got older, two things became crystal clear. Although her aunt Lois never had anything bad to say about Phire's father, she'd never said anything good about him, either. There had definitely been a disconnect in the brother-sister relationship. Granted, there was a fourteen-year difference in their ages, but Phire would have thought they'd have a closer sibling bond.

More than once she'd tried getting her aunt to talk about it, but she never would. The only thing Aunt Lois would say, was that whatever was done in the dark would eventually come to light. Phire often wondered what she meant. Another thing her aunt had warned her about was to never to cross him.

When Phire finished high school at seventeen, her father had finally sent for her, saying he wanted her to attend an American university. After college, Phire decided to make her home in Paris, and at the age of twenty-one, nothing her father did or said could make her change her mind. She reminded him that she was now an adult and old enough to make her own decisions. Besides, why would he want her around when he hadn't before?

After she'd been living back in Paris for a year, her aunt had a massive stroke, which left her without speech and paralyzed in the legs. That meant Aunt Lois was in need of constant attention in a long-term care facility. When the funds for Aunt Lois's care ran out, a frantic Phire had no other choice but to reach out to her father, convinced he would come to his sister's aid.

Simon Bordella had agreed to provide the funds for his sister's care, but not out of the goodness of his heart. He'd told Phire that he would only agree to help on one condition—Phire would agree to marry whatever man he chose for her without any questions asked.

At first, Phire thought he was joking. When she saw he was not, she was appalled. It was only when the doctors stressed what could happen to her aunt without proper long-term care that, out of desperation, Phire agreed to her father's terms.

"I asked, where do you think you're going, Sapphire?"

She turned around. "I need to think, and I can't do it here."

"What is there to think about? I kept my end of

the agreement and provided the best care possible for Lois. Now it's time you kept your end of the deal."

Phire narrowed her gaze at him. "I had hoped you wouldn't hold that agreement over my head. I'd begun thinking that you were providing the best of care to Aunt Lois because she is your sister."

"Well, you thought wrong. Lois and I never got along. The only reason I've been paying those exorbitant fees for three years is because of the deal you and I made."

"Why, Dad? Why is it important for you to select the man for me to marry?"

"The reason doesn't matter. All you need to know is that now that you're twenty-five, it's time for you to settle down and Jaxon Ravnell will make the perfect son-in-law."

Phire frowned as she thought of the man she'd been introduced to last night at dinner. "Why? Because he's wealthy and you think he can be easily manipulated?"

Her father smiled as if he found what she'd said amusing. "Jaxon does have more money than he knows what to do with, so what's wrong with me helping him decide the best way to use it?"

Phire didn't say anything. She would admit that thirty-two-year-old Jaxon was definitely a handsome man. He was the CEO of several technology firms in Virginia and was in Texas looking for land to expand. Her father had met him a few weeks ago at one of those Texas business meetings, where the red carpet had practically been rolled out for Jaxon.

Over dinner last night her father had tried his

hardest to sell Jaxon on the idea that he needed to invest some of his millions by buying up a lot of the land in the area. Mainly land her father owned that was adjacent to the ranch.

She'd always been good at reading people, and it had been obvious to her—even if hadn't been to her father—that Jaxon *wasn't* a man who could be easily manipulated. For some reason, she had a feeling Jaxon was actually playing her father by pretending the opposite. That was something she found rather interesting.

What her father had said earlier was true. He had made sure her aunt had the best of care in one of the finest facilities in Paris. He had kept his end of their deal, and whether she wanted to or not, she would keep hers.

"I need you back here in two days, Sapphire. I could tell over dinner that Jaxon was taken with you. He said he'd be in the area for at least six months and you two should spend time together. I want a wedding to take place no later than the spring. Understood?"

When she didn't say anything, he continued, "Just in case you don't understand, maybe now is the time to tell you that I had Lois moved."

"You did what?" she asked furiously, crossing the room to her father.

"You heard me. Just in case you try to wiggle out of our agreement. Don't worry, my sister is still getting the best of care, just in a nondisclosed location. I won't tell you where until *after* you and Jaxon get married."

"You can't do that!"

"As her legal guardian, I can do whatever I want. Don't worry about your aunt. What you need to concern yourself with is getting Jaxon to make you his wife by spring. As far as I'm concerned, there's nothing you need to think about. However, if you feel the need to get away to accept your fate, then by all means, do so. But I expect you back in two days with a smile on your face, ready to convince Jaxon that you are the best thing that could ever happen to him."

When her father walked out the room, Phire sank down on the bed.

Maverick checked his watch as he paced the confines of the hotel room. He hadn't expected to arrive in Dallas before Phire and had texted her all the information she needed, including the fact that a hotel key in her name was at the check-in desk.

He knew everyone was wondering why he'd left Denver unexpectedly, when he and his brothers had planned to remain in Westmoreland Country for another two days. His brother Sloan had made a wisecrack that it must have something to do with a woman. His brother was right on that account. What Sloan was wrong about was in thinking this was a hookup.

Maverick considered Phire more than that.

From their first meeting it had been easy to see she was unlike any woman he'd ever known. In addition to her striking beauty, she had wit and a personality that drew him even when he hadn't wanted to be drawn. And the more he had gotten to know her, the more he'd appreciated their friendship. Entering into a FWB relationship had been the first of its kind for him. Before Phire, he would never have considered such a thing.

As he waited for her arrival, he couldn't help but recall when they'd first met. It had been his and Garth's second night in Paris, and Maverick had decided to check out the nightlife at a pub someone had recommended. Since the place was a few blocks away and it had been a beautiful night in April, he'd walked.

As Maverick gazed out the hotel window at downtown Dallas, he let himself remember when he'd met Sapphire Bordella. It was a night he would never forget…

Two

Paris, France
Three years ago

"Welcome to DuRands. What can I get you?" the bartender asked when Maverick slid onto the barstool.

"Brandy," he said easily.

"Bottle or glass?" the woman responded with a grin.

Maverick couldn't help but return her amusement. Nor could he help noticing how gorgeous she was as he studied her with deep male appreciation. He had an eye for beauty and on a scale of one to ten, he gave her a twenty plus. She was stunning, and that said a lot since he'd met a number of striking women in his lifetime.

She wore little makeup and her mass of dark brown curls cascaded around her face, complementing her mocha skin tone. He didn't have to see the lower part of her to figure the rest of her looked just as sexy. And damn, she smelled good, too. He might have been bored to tears while attending those business meetings earlier today, but his interest was now piqued at the highest level. He'd never hit on a bartender before but there was a first time for everything.

"Do I look stressed enough for a bottle?" he asked, grinning, and noticed there was no ring on her left hand. He didn't believe in encroaching on another man's territory. A boyfriend who wasn't smart enough to put a ring on her finger was of no significance.

The woman tilted her head to the left and then to the right as if closely scrutinizing him, then said, "Not stressed, but you look like you have plenty of time to kill."

"I do, but if I tackle a bottle you might have to carry me out of here."

"I don't have a problem carrying you anywhere, mister," she said, flashing a pair of the most beautiful dimples he'd ever seen.

A crackle of energy passed between them with her words. He'd had women flirt with him before. However, there was something about *this* woman that had everything within him standing at attention… which meant it was a good thing he was sitting down.

"I need to know the name of the person who might end up rescuing me from a drunken stupor," he said, liking how the opening of her shirt hinted at a pair of awesome breasts.

She smiled again and a burst of need hit his stomach. "I'm Sapphire Bordella. However, my friends call me Phire."

"Phire," he said, liking how easily her name rolled off his lips. It was pronounced the same, but spelled differently from one of the classical elements. The one he was feeling now, burning him.

"And what's yours?" she asked.

"Maverick Outlaw."

She nodded. "Maverick. I like that. And are you one or the other? A maverick or an outlaw?"

He chuckled. "My family claims I am both, and from my escapades that often get me into trouble, I have no reason not to believe them."

She grinned. "Then I definitely need to keep my eyes on you tonight, Maverick, the outlaw."

"What about you? Are you a precious gem or are you as hot as the name *Phire* implies?"

She gave him one of those smiles that made a jolt of sexual energy rock him to the core. And her skin… He was tempted to reach across the bar and touch it to see if it was as soft as it looked. "I'll claim both. With that said, I'll be back with your drink."

Maverick watched her walk off, thinking he would definitely keep his eyes on her as well. It didn't take her long to return with his glass of brandy and their hands touched. Another jolt of sexual energy hit him. It had been his intent to grab a table to enjoy the live band, but he'd rather stay sitting right here at the bar and get to know Phire better. All he had was her name, but he definitely wanted more.

His brother Sloan had once called Maverick a man-whore, which hadn't hurt his feelings any. He liked women. They liked him. He didn't believe in lingering in any woman's bed for more than a few nights. He detested a clingy woman or one who thought a romp between the sheets came with certain rights. He was quick to remind them that it did not.

"So, are you American or French?" he asked, since he detected both accents in her words but couldn't tell which was more dominate.

She glanced up from wiping off the counter. "American. Born in the heart of Texas. I assume you're American, although you have an accent I can't place."

"I was born in Alaska and still live there. In fact, my first trip to the lower forty-eight wasn't until I graduated from high school. I got my own plane and flew there myself."

"You own a plane and can fly it?"

He heard the amazement in her voice. He often used that tidbit as a conversation starter with women. The interest drew them in every time. "Yes. Due to Alaska's limited road system, the most common way for us to get around is by personal aircraft."

She smiled. "That's interesting."

"How long have you been living in Paris?" he asked, taking a sip of his brandy.

"I moved here when I was twelve, not long after my mother died. I guess my father thought raising a daughter was more than he wanted to take on, so he sent me to his older sister. I lived with Aunt Lois until I graduated from high school at seventeen. Then Dad sent for me because he wanted me to attend college in Texas."

"Where?"

"University of Texas in Austin. The day after I graduated, I returned here."

Maverick took another sip, finding her story interesting. Her father had sent her away at twelve, but his own father had had a different mindset. Bart hadn't minded raising five sons alone. "Do you still live with your aunt?"

"Aunt Lois had a massive stroke earlier this year that left her paralyzed. She's currently in a long-term-care facility."

"I'm sorry to hear that."

"Thanks. Excuse me, I've got another customer."

He nodded and watched her talk to the guy who'd just arrived. From her greeting, the man was someone she knew. Possibly a regular. She proved the assumption right when she didn't ask the man what he wanted to drink. She knew.

She remained at the other end of the bar, chatting with the guy, and a part of Maverick felt peeved. He frowned. Lack of attention from a woman had never annoyed him before, so why did it now? Maybe because she could ignore him, but he couldn't ignore her. There was something about that soft-looking skin, that curly hair and those gorgeous dark eyes, that had him mesmerized.

A half hour later, she came back down to his end of the bar to see if he wanted more brandy. He said he did and while she was pouring, he asked, "You don't look old enough to be a bartender. How long have you been one?"

She smiled up at him. "I'm twenty-two and actually I'm not a bartender. At least not usually. The couple who owns this club are the parents of a good friend of mine. Their regular bartender called in sick so they asked if I could help out."

"You're good at it."

"Thanks. During my summers while in college, I would return to Paris and work here as a waitress. On those slow days, I learned the art of being a bartender. The DuRands know they can call me if they ever need help."

"And what do you do when you're not helping out here?"

"I work at a clothing boutique."

"Do you find that interesting?"

She chuckled. "I find anything having to do with clothes interesting. One day I plan to open my own shop."

"And I'm sure you will." He glanced at his watch. "What time do you get off tonight, Phire?"

She lifted an eyebrow. "Why?"

"I'd like to get to know you better. Thought we could grab a table over there and listen to the band."

She nodded, which to him meant she didn't have a problem with his suggestion. "The club closes at midnight, but I'm only needed until ten." She studied his features for a minute and then said, "And I'd like to get to know you better, too, Maverick, the outlaw."

While pouring a drink for another customer, Phire couldn't help but glance over at the man she'd flirted with off and on for most of the night. There was no reason to pretend she didn't find him irresistible, because she did. And he was a great conversationalist.

She didn't want to think about all the men she'd gone out with who had bored her to tears.

She glanced at the clock and saw that in ten minutes, her shift ended. A part of her couldn't wait. She had noticed Maverick Outlaw the minute he had walked into the club—he was any woman's fantasy man.

He had to be every bit of six foot two and was handsome as sin. She wasn't sure what attracted her more, the darkness of his eyes, the slash of his eyebrows, the smooth coppery brown of his skin, the shape of his lips or that panty-wetting cleft in his chin. Or it could be that sexy-looking beard on his jaw. Another thing she'd noticed was how observant his gaze was. It had been on her most of the night and she hoped he liked what he saw.

She would admit he was the first man to not only grab her attention, but also to hold it. After her high school sweetheart, Jacques Fontaine, had broken her heart, she'd sworn she wouldn't become seriously involved with a man again. For the last four years, she'd done just that.

When she'd left Paris for college, Jacques had promised to wait for her, that she was worth the long-distance romance they would endure. By the end of her freshman year, his calls became infrequent. Then she had gotten the dreaded letter. Unfortunately, the letter hadn't reached her until his wedding day.

The lessons she'd learned from that heartbreak were to never engage in a long-distance romance and to never give her heart to another man.

The moment Maverick told her he was from Alaska and in Paris on business, she had checked off one of her "never do" boxes. Otherwise, not falling for him would be a challenge. He was a man a woman could give her heart to without a second thought.

"I'm here, Phire."

She glanced up and smiled at Clancy DuRand, the guy who'd been her good friend since the first year she'd moved to Paris. "Good, because I have a date."

He chuckled. "You mean that guy at the bar who hasn't taken his eyes off you for the past couple of hours."

She grinned. "Were you watching me through that one-sided mirror your father installed?"

Clancy smiled. "Of course. I've always looked out for you and old habits are hard to break."

"Whatever. Just for spying on me, you can start a few minutes early while I go get ready for my date."

"Who's the guy?"

"No one you have to worry about. By the way, how's Dionne?" she asked, wondering about his wife.

"She looks like a woman who's about to have twins."

Phire laughed. "She is a woman who *will* be having twins, dude."

"Don't remind me."

"I didn't. You brought it up, and I don't know why you're so worried. You're going to make a great dad to daughters."

"I hope so."

"You will. You got plenty of practice trying to keep up with me in school. Now hold down the fort and don't you dare interrogate my date or I'll never speak to you again."

"So you say."

"So I mean, Clancy." With that said, she handed him the bar towel and walked toward the back. She didn't have to glance over her shoulder to know Clancy was already making his way over to where Maverick was sitting. To interrogate him.

The loft above DuRands was where Clancy had lived before marrying Dionne and it was still unoccupied. It didn't take Phire long to use the facilities there to shower and change into another outfit. Then she released her hair from the knot on her head and applied new lipstick. Satisfied with her appearance, she left to join Maverick. He had turned around on his stool to take in the band getting into their third number. She would know since they were regulars and rarely changed their routine.

Maverick couldn't have heard her approach over the sound of the loud music, but he turned his head to look at her. His gaze was so penetrating she almost missed a step, and she was not one to be clumsy.

Phire never had a man look at her with such intensity. Total awareness of him seeped into every pore. She was aroused just from seeing him sitting on that stool, from being aware of the full length of him, from the top of his head to the soles of those expensive-looking shoes. And when he stood, he was taller than she'd originally assumed.

"I'm here," she said, when she finally reached him. She had to tilt back her head to meet his gaze.

He did a thorough sweep of her outfit before meeting her eyes again. "You changed clothes."

"I usually keep a change of clothes here," she said.

"That's convenient."

"For me, it's a necessity. The shop where I work is in the next block. I live quite a way from here and on those days that I prefer hanging out with friends or going to check on my aunt, it's easier for me to shower and change here than go all the way home and then come back."

"That makes sense."

"How did you know I was approaching? You must have awfully good hearing."

He smiled. "No, I picked up your scent."

"Oh." No man had ever told her something like that before.

"You want to find a place to sit?" he asked.

"I'd rather not. You've heard three of the band's numbers already, and I've been here for five hours. I need a change of scenery."

He cocked his head and looked at her. "Then where would you prefer going?"

She could tell from the look in his eyes what he was thinking. Having Clancy as a good friend helped since he'd been quite the rascal before meeting Dionne. "I missed dinner and I'm starving. It just so happens that my favorite café is right across the street. While I eat, you can tell me about all those bad things you've done to earn you the last name of Outlaw."

It didn't take Maverick long to know that he liked Phire, and not just because he desperately wanted her in his bed. He was enjoying his time with her. Just watching her eat was a total turn-on. Nobody ate French onion soup quite the way she did. Each time she brought the spoon to her lips was sensuality in motion.

"So there you have it," he said, continuing their conversation. "I was the youngest of five brothers and I wanted attention any way I could get it."

"So you were a real rascal."

He chuckled. "Yes, I'll admit that I was." He took a sip of his wine, and then said, "Clancy is your protector, I gather."

She chuckled. "He's the brother I always wanted is more like it. On my first day in school here in Paris, I was twelve and scared to death. He assured me everything would be alright. I believed him since he was the only one in my class who spoke English."

Maverick couldn't help but chuckle again. He'd been doing that a lot tonight. Not only was Phire gorgeous, but she was also entertaining. He had eaten dinner earlier with Garth and Regan, who had flown them both here as the company pilot, so he'd only ordered a glass of wine when Phire had ordered her soup.

"I hope Clancy didn't drill you too much," Phire said, interrupting his thoughts.

"I didn't mind. I have a younger sister, too. Charm is twenty-five."

"And you and your brothers get all into her business, right?"

"There was a time when we did, but we soon discovered Charm could take care of herself."

That was an understatement. Bart hadn't known Claudia was pregnant when their affair had ended and she left for parts unknown. Fifteen years later, she'd reappeared with Charm in tow, telling Bart that she couldn't handle Charm's sassiness anymore. He could deal with it. Bart's way of dealing with it had been to spoil Charm even more. That's when the brothers had taken a firm hand to their newly discovered sister. In the end, Charm had settled down. Thanks to her five older brothers, she definitely knew how to handle herself without their interference.

"So tell me about your life in Texas, Phire."

She shrugged beautiful shoulders barely covered by the cute blouse she was wearing. The moment he'd picked up her scent and turned to look at her in the sexy outfit she'd changed into, his breath had caught on a surge of desire so strong he'd wondered if he'd be capable of breathing again.

"My father, Simon Bordella, used to be an attorney in my grandfather's law practice. After my grandfather died, Dad sold the practice, stopped practicing law and tried his hand at ranching. All this took place before I was born." She paused. "I would love Texas more if my father wasn't such a tyrant."

Maverick lifted an eyebrow. "His name isn't Bart, is it?"

She smiled. "No, his name is Simon and there's nothing simple about him, trust me." She took a sip of her wine then asked, "I take it that your father, Bart, is a tyrant as well."

"Worse. But my siblings and I have learned how to deal with him."

"By just letting him have his way?"

"Hell no. Just the opposite. That doesn't mean he doesn't try. He's one manipulating old cuss."

"You say that with fondness and not an ounce of bitterness."

"It won't do any good. We understand Bart, or we try to."

"What about your sister? Does he treat her worse?"

Maverick rolled his eyes. "Hardly. Charm's the apple of the old man's eye. Definitely a daddy's girl."

He'd told Phire more about himself and his family than he normally would tell a woman, especially on a first date. And he did consider this a date. However, whether it ended with him in her bed, or her in his, was yet to be seen.

"I'll never understand my father."

He came close to telling her that at some point she would need to let it go. She was a grown woman living in Paris, thousands of miles away from Texas, so why did it matter if she understood her old man or not? For years, Maverick hadn't understood his mother, Rosalind. She'd been Bart's wife, whom he'd caught in an affair. Lucky for Maverick, there hadn't been any question that he'd been Bart's kid since he favored the old man more than any of the others. Right down to the cleft in his chin.

He glanced at his watch and saw it was close to midnight. He had intended to be in some woman's bed tonight and had hoped it would be Phire's. "It's getting late," he finally said.

"I know." She smiled over at him after she pushed aside her empty bowl. "So tell me, Maverick, the outlaw. Are you going to see me home like a nice gentleman would?"

Three

The sound of a muffler backfiring brought Maverick's thoughts back to the present. He was still staring out the hotel window. Christmas decorations were everywhere, and he found it hard to believe that Thanksgiving was next week.

He couldn't help recalling how that night with Phire had ended. After leaving the café, they had walked back to his hotel. Then he'd gotten the rental car and driven her home. Her car, she'd told him, was in the shop and she would be picking it up tomorrow. She had planned to take a rideshare home.

Phire had been right when she'd said she lived outside the city limits. He thought the stucco home, nestled among smaller chateaus in the countryside, was a really nice place. He especially liked the garden courtyard that led to her front door.

She'd told him her aunt had lived in the house for years and how lonely it was without her aunt's presence. He knew from all the things she'd said that her relationship with her aunt was a close one, and other than her father, her aunt was the only living relative she had.

He had walked Phire to the door, and she'd invited him inside. Not one to waste time on formalities, the moment the door closed behind them, he had drawn her into his arms. The moment their mouths had connected, he'd been a goner.

That night they'd made love after she'd told him she had never done anything so promiscuous before—inviting a man she barely knew home for the night. She'd even told him that she hadn't shared a bed with a man in over four years and why. He knew all about the heartbreak she'd endured upon receiving her boyfriend's letter on the day of his wedding to another woman.

Another thing Phire had done before sharing a bed with Maverick was set the ground rules, which was something he usually did with women. She'd made it clear that the night with him would be just a night. She didn't do long-distance, long-term or long-lasting. In other words, they would be one and done.

By the next morning, he was convinced Phire had gotten under his skin in a way no other woman had. That night had started their friendship with benefits, which had continued for two years. He would hook up with her whenever he came to Paris, and he'd made it his business to return often.

During his visits, he'd often accompanied her to movies, concerts and dinners. He'd even gone with her to visit her aunt Lois. He knew how much she cared about her aunt. The older woman was in a very nice facility and definitely well cared for.

Phire had told him that her father was footing the bill for all her aunt's expenses. Maverick thought that no matter how much of a tyrant the man was, at least he'd had the decency to take care of his sister.

He rubbed his hand down his face while thinking that the real kick in the gut had come last year, when Phire suggested they end their FWB relationship. She wanted to start dating seriously. He'd been surprised since she'd sworn she would never fall in love again. But he knew she had a right to change her mind. After all, his brothers, Garth and Cash, whom he'd thought would never marry, had done so.

Maverick knew that although he wasn't in love with Phire and she wasn't in love with him, there was a bond between them. That's why he was here in Dallas. It didn't matter that their FWB relationship had ended over a year ago, and he hadn't spoken with her but a few times since. The bottom line was that she'd called and said she needed to see him, and he was here.

He turned around when he heard the key in the door. His heart rate increased as he watched it open. And there she stood. The woman he had thought about over the last year more than he should have.

The look on her face had him quickly crossing the room to gather her into his arms.

* * *

Phire inhaled deeply when she was enveloped in Maverick's warm embrace. He was the man who'd turned her world inside out within months of meeting him. His familiar scent calmed her in ways he would never know. He was the last person she should have called, but she hadn't been able to *not* call him.

"What's wrong, Phire?"

At that moment, Phire couldn't speak. Nor did she want to. The only thing she wanted was for Maverick to hold her while she buried her head on his chest and fought back her tears.

She had tried putting distance between them at the first sign she was developing feelings for him. That's when she'd come up with the big lie that she needed space to start dating others. Falling in love with him would have made things hard because of that agreement she'd made with her father.

Her future was not her own so there was no reason for her to have any fanciful hope of anything ever growing between her and Maverick. Besides, he didn't love her. The only thing they'd shared for those two years was a friendship with benefits. There was no doubt in her mind that they still would be FWB if she hadn't ended things.

The thought of how miserable she'd been over the last year without Maverick made tears well up in her eyes. Her aunt's condition wasn't improving, and the doctors had told her to stop holding on to hope that it would. However, it had been enough for her aunt to recognize her during her visits and give her a smile. Phire had looked forward to that smile. Now, thanks to her father, she had no idea where her aunt was. Did her aunt know why Phire no longer visited her? The thought made more tears come.

"What's wrong, Phire? Please tell me."

Until Maverick had spoken, she hadn't realized she'd been sobbing into his chest. But she hadn't been able to help it. For two years he had been her strength. He'd been what was right in her world when everything else seemed to be tumbling down all around her.

When she didn't say anything, she suddenly felt herself being swept off her feet into Maverick's strong arms and carried over to the sofa. Maverick had booked a suite, and she'd noticed how big it was the minute she'd opened the door.

Cradling her in his arms, he held her tight while gently stroking her back. "Talk to me, Phire. Did you and that guy break up or something?"

She lifted her head, swiped at her tears and asked, "What guy?"

"The one you ended our relationship to begin seeing."

"There was never a guy."

He looked at her strangely and said, "Oh."

Realizing what she'd just admitted, she quickly said, "I never got around to meeting anyone. I was too busy."

He nodded. "Then has something happened to your aunt? Is that the reason you're back in the States for a while?"

She saw the depth of concern in the darkness of his eyes. He didn't love her, but their friendship had always been solid. She knew he genuinely cared.

Pulling herself up, she straightened in his lap and wiped the tears from her eyes. "I'm sorry. I should not have fallen apart like that."

"You don't have to apologize for letting go if you needed to. I'm Maverick, remember?"

There was no way she could forget. He was Maverick, her outlaw. But he was also more. He was the man who had become her world even when he hadn't known it. She had looked forward to his visits, no matter how infrequent they'd become. He was a treat worth waiting for.

She had given him a key to her place, and there was nothing like coming home from work to find him there. They would spend time together as friends and lovers. Maverick had a way about him that had her laughing at his antics one minute and screaming out his name in an orgasm the next. Their relationship had been unique. It had been special. Even Clancy had said as much. He had accused her of falling in love with Maverick even before she'd realized she was doing so.

"Yes, it's about Aunt Lois."

He nodded as he gently stroked the side of her face. "And?"

She fought back more tears. "I don't know where she is."

He frowned and then tilted his head to look at her with a confused expression. "How can you not know where she is? Is she not in that facility in Paris?"

Phire shook her head "Dad moved her and won't tell me where she is."

"Why would he do that?"

"Because he needs to make sure I keep my end of the deal and marry the man he's picked up for me."

Holding her steadily in his arms, Maverick straightened up in his seat. "I think you need to start from the beginning, Phire."

Although Maverick was trying like hell to hold his anger in check, he was having a hard time doing so. First, he was furious at Phire's father for asking her to agree to something so outlandish. The other part of his anger was directed at her. Not for agreeing to the arrangement, because he figured she would do anything to give her aunt the best of care, but that she hadn't told him anything about it until now.

"Why am I just hearing about this crazy-ass deal you made with your father, Phire?" he asked, not caring if she heard the harshness in his tone. It couldn't be helped, since he was fuming.

"It happened before I met you. In fact, it was the month before. I didn't even mention it to Clancy. All I was concerned with was making sure Aunt Lois received the best care."

She twisted in his lap to face him fully. "I honestly was hoping Dad would see how ridiculous his ultimatum was. And that helping with his sister's health care was the decent thing to do. I was wrong. My dad doesn't have a decent bone in his body. He's been biding his time and waiting for the right prospect to come along."

"So you're going to marry the man he picked?" he asked incredulously.

"What choice do I have, Maverick? If I don't then

I might never see Aunt Lois again. Not knowing where she is, it's tearing me up inside."

He pulled Phire into his arms and held her when the tears began to fall again. Simon Bordella was an ass, not deserving to have Phire for a daughter or her aunt Lois as a sister.

"I understand, Phire, but at some point you'll need to stand up to him. After living with Bart for thirty-two years, I've learned that the only way to deal with a wannabe dictator is to stand up to them once and for all."

"I want to but I can't, Maverick. There's too much at stake. There is no doubt in my mind that if I don't give Dad what he wants I won't see Aunt Lois again."

"How can you even deal with the thought of what he's demanding that you do?"

"By reminding myself that I did agree to the deal. As crazy as Dad's ultimatum sounds, and I'll forever think he did it for the wrong reasons, he kept his end of the agreement. You've even commented about how nice a place it was where Aunt Lois was being kept." She paused while swiping at her eyes. "Then there's Jaxon Ravnell."

He lifted an eyebrow. "Who's Jaxon Ravnell?"

"The man Dad has chosen for me to marry. Dad invited Jaxon to dinner the first day I arrived home, and practically every single evening since. He honestly seems like a nice guy, and I think he's fully aware Dad is trying to throw us together. My orders are to convince Jaxon that I'm the best thing for him."

She paused again. "For some reason I think Jaxon is pretending to be easily persuadable, but he has no intention of letting Dad railroad him. There's something about Jaxon that makes me thinks he's playing Dad."

Maverick didn't say anything for a minute. If what she believed was true, then her father deserved it. What Phire didn't deserve was to be caught in the middle. "I still think you should stand up to your father."

"As long as I don't know where Aunt Lois is, I can't and he knows it." She added, "I'm hoping Jaxon found me not to his liking, anyway."

As far as Maverick was concerned, unless this Ravnell guy was blind, there was no way he hadn't thought Phire was beautiful.

"I don't want to talk about Dad and Jaxon anymore," she said. "I've missed you, Maverick. We haven't talked in almost a year. To be honest, I wasn't sure you would even take my call."

He looked down at her. "Why?"

"Because we agreed to end our FWB relationship."

"Do I need to remind you it was your idea, Phire?" He wouldn't tell her that they shared a bond he couldn't explain and an intense attraction he couldn't deny. Whenever he thought of her in the arms of another guy, it was like a knife being driven in his heart. He kept telling himself there should be no reason for him to feel that way when he didn't love her, but the feeling persisted nonetheless. Over the last year, he had thrown himself into his work, trying to get over her. He'd finally taken off a couple of weeks in August, when he had gone to visit his cousins in Napa Valley.

Instead of responding to what he'd said, she cuddled in his arms, and he held her as neither said anything else. For a minute he thought she had dozed off with him holding her. Then she shifted in his lap to gaze up at him again. The moment their eyes connected, he felt it. That crackle of energy that would pass between them when desire simmered, making the air hot and raw with need.

Whenever that happened, he became aware of how she felt in his arms, the heat of her skin and her scent. Especially her scent. He heard it when her breath caught, almost at the same time as his. He felt a yearning so sexual that his entire body began to ache.

"Phire."

He whispered her name as she leaned up and offered him her lips for a taste of what he knew was the sweetest, most delicious flavor any mouth could possess. At that moment, he could no more not give her what they both wanted than he could stop breathing.

"I have to give Dad what he wants, Maverick, so tonight has to be goodbye," she whispered when he brought his lips closer to hers.

Like hell it would be. There was no way he would allow her father to force her into marrying anyone. When she stuck out her tongue to lick his lips, his guts twisted, and he captured her mouth in his. He heard the low moan from deep within her throat and it did something to him. He hadn't heard it in a long time and had missed the sound of it.

Their kiss intensified and he became aware of her in every pore of his body, in every single cell. Somehow, he managed to ease off the sofa with her still cradled in his arms and their lips remaining locked. He broke off the kiss, and whispered the words, "I want you, Phire."

"I want you, too," she responded.

Satisfied that their thoughts, wants and needs were in sync, Maverick headed toward the bedroom.

Phire had meant what she'd told Maverick. She wanted him. She'd also meant it when she said this would be goodbye. She couldn't fight her father, not if she wanted to find out the location of her aunt. What if Jaxon didn't want to marry her any more than she wanted to marry him?

But all other thoughts left her mind the moment Maverick placed her on the huge bed. And then he stepped back and stared at her. He would never know just how much she loved him. It didn't matter if she ended up marrying Jaxon or some other man. Maverick Outlaw would always have her heart.

"Earlier you said you missed me. Well, I've missed you, too, Phire. I missed talking to you on the phone, flying to Paris knowing when I got there that I would see you, spend time with you, make love to you. I missed the sound of you breathing, inhaling your scent. I missed everything about you."

Whether Maverick knew it or not, his words touched her deeply, although she knew they were based on lust and not love. It didn't matter. Just knowing he'd come when she'd called meant everything to her. This was the goodbye she needed.

"I'm here now, Maverick. Please don't keep me waiting."

There could never be an emotional aspect to their relationship, but they'd always had the physical. But then, at present, they weren't even *in* a relationship. They weren't even friends who shared benefits. They were friends who had to say goodbye. Unlike when they'd ended their FWB relationship, and they had kept in touch. At least for a while. Until it had become painful to hear his voice. That's when she'd decided to fade from his life and let him assume she'd met someone else.

This time when they parted it would be permanent. She wouldn't be able to call Maverick again just to see him, be held by him. By then she would be someone else's wife.

Phire watched as he moved toward the bed, then sat on it to remove his shoes and socks. Afterward, he removed her boots and socks, gently easing them off.

"You have beautiful feet," he said throatily.

"Thanks. You have beautiful feet, too."

Maverick did and she would often tell him that. He reached for her and she came willingly, knowing he enjoyed undressing her. And she always loved the way he did it, because as he removed each piece he let her know how much he liked every inch of her body. Tonight was no exception.

When she was completely naked, he stood and stared at her. She sat back on her haunches in the middle of the bed and smiled up at him. Maverick, her outlaw. "Now it's my turn."

"Okay."

She scooted across the bed to him and began unbuttoning his shirt, taking her time. Knowing this would be the last time she performed this ritual made her chest fill with anguish and she fought back a sob. She loved him and she had to give him up. The last time she'd done so, she'd known that although she was giving up the benefits, there would always be the friendship. That wouldn't be the case anymore.

When she had finished with the last button, she eased the shirt off a pair of massive shoulders. She then gazed at the naked chest she loved. "Now for your pants. As usual, I'm going to need your help." She always had a problem sliding his pants down his aroused body.

"No problem," he said in a voice that was huskier than usual. She eased off the bed and went to him. Together they tackled the removal of his pants and then he stood before her as naked as she was.

Maverick pulled her into his arms and together they tumbled back on the bed as he covered her mouth with his.

Four

With his kiss, Maverick wanted Phire to know just how much he had missed her.

He had assumed she would be out of sight and out of mind, but she hadn't been. And no other woman he'd been with since they'd been apart had eradicated her from beneath his skin. He'd missed her taste and the way heat ignited between them before they could draw in another breath. Passion had always been more than within their reach. It took control with an intensity that had them both moaning before things even got started.

Like now.

The mating of their mouths seemed endless, as if they were making up for lost time. Over a year's worth. He continued to kiss her, hungrily, greedily, needing this as much as he needed to take another breath.

When oxygen finally became a necessity, he broke off the kiss and rested his forehead against hers, breathing deeply. Mentally, he knew he needed to slow down, but physically, he wasn't sure he could. He gently stroked the bare skin of her neck, before leaning in to lick the area, loving how her skin tasted.

"Maverick…"

"Yes, baby?" he answered.

He had gotten aroused even more from hearing her say his name. He skimmed his fingers over her upper body, reacquainting himself with her breasts. He cupped them in his palms. Lowering his head, he swiped his tongue across her nipples several times before covering a breast with his mouth to suck hard on it. Her body shivered beneath his mouth and that only made his erection harder.

"Two can play your game, Maverick, the outlaw."

Before he realized her intent, she pushed him on his back, her warm hands claiming just what she wanted. "It's been a while, Notorious," she said, talking to his throbbing member and referring to it by the name she'd given it. "Before you show me how much you've missed me, let me show you how much I've missed, you, too."

With that said, she eased him into her mouth while her fingers stroked his sensitive flesh. The loud moan that escaped his lips couldn't be helped. Nor could he stop himself from groaning her name and clenching the bed coverings. And when she ardently worked her mouth on him, he felt as if he was being driven out of his mind.

Over and over again, she brought him to the verge of ecstasy, and when he felt ready to explode, she refused to let go. She deliberately clamped her mouth down on Notorious while her tongue got greedier.

"Phire!"

He let loose and she still refused to let go. When he managed to regain the sanity he'd lost to her mouth, he flipped their bodies.

He was about to thrust into her when she said, "Wait. I'm no longer on the pill."

He went still and stared down at her. "Why not?"

"I began getting headaches, so the doctor took me off them for a while. I didn't have a problem with that since I was no longer sexually active."

He nodded, eased off the bed and picked up his pants off the floor. "No problem. I've got condoms."

"Good." The mass of brown hair that covered her head was in disarray around her shoulders and the eyes staring back at him were filled with as much desire as he was feeling.

He smiled as he went back to her. "Since you wanted to get a taste of me, now is my time to get one of you," he said, scooting back onto the bed. Before she could close her legs, his head was between them.

His greedy tongue took delight in giving absolute attention to her clit. He knew she was feeling good when she lifted her hips off the bed and held tight to his head to keep him there. It wasn't long before he had licked her right into an orgasm.

Then he moved on top of her, groaning in anticipation. He went deep, and deeper still. Her inner muscles held him tight, trying to take him hostage, but he pulled back and began thrusting hard. Over and over again, refusing to let up or slow down.

He kept going and going and when she screamed his name, he let go. Thrusting harder, he felt the moment his semen released inside her.

What the hell!

Although it had never happened to him before, he knew that it had this time. Damn! The condom had broken and Notorious was living up to his name. And Phire felt like fire. She didn't know what had happened, and he was about to tell her when he felt her inner muscles tightening around Notorious even more, milking everything out of him. She was doing a damn good job. Too good. He was about to pull out of her, but then his treacherous body responded and bucked straight into another orgasm. When she screamed out his name, he knew she had reached another high as well.

It was only when they were sated that he eased off her and pulled her into his arms. He glanced over at her and saw that her eyes were closed and her lips were spread into a satisfied smile.

"Phire?"

"Hmm…"

"Open your eyes, baby. There's something I need to tell you."

She evidently heard something in his voice that had her slowly opening her eyes and looking at him. "What?"

"The condom broke."

* * *

Maverick held Phire while she slept. After the shock had worn off from his words, she'd said it wasn't the right time of the month for her to get pregnant. That relieved his fears…somewhat.

Since she didn't seem bothered by the accident, he tried not to be, either. He'd gone to the bathroom and dispensed of the defective condom. Since all the ones in his wallet had come from the same package, he had left her sleeping while he'd put on his clothes and gone downstairs to the hotel's gift shop to purchase a new pack.

She'd told him she wanted to spend the next two days with him, and he wanted to make sure he not only had enough condoms, but that they were also ones he could depend on. Like he'd told her, nothing like that had ever happened to him before.

He doubted she knew just how good it felt having her back in his arms. Since ending their FWB relationship, he'd tried returning to his routine of being a perpetual womanizer but had discovered he couldn't. At least not to the degree that he had been before Phire. He'd found other women lacking.

Now, he glanced down at Phire and smiled at how her lips tilted at a seductive angle as she slept. Sleeping or awake, the woman was totally alluring. He recalled what she'd said about not being involved with anyone during the year they'd parted. She would never know how many nights he'd lain awake thinking about her. Phire was everything any man would need. Not only was she gorgeous, but she was also intelligent, thoughtful, loving and kind, which was evidenced by how she looked out for her aunt. There was no doubt in his mind that some lucky guy would appreciate having her on his arm. *In his arms.*

He hated admitting it, but deep down, part of him was glad she hadn't found her Mr. Right. He didn't fully understand why he felt that way, but the thought of her with another man cut him to the core.

Maverick had convinced himself it wasn't jealousy that made him feel that way. It was merely the fact that she was his friend, and he didn't want any man to ever hurt her again like that prick Jacques Fontaine had done.

And that included her father.

There had to be something he could do. Even if it meant contacting his cousins, Quade and Cole Westmoreland. The two owned a security firm with international connections. Maybe they could find out where Phire's father had moved her aunt. Hopefully, Quade and Cole could even give an update on the woman's condition. That information could definitely give Phire peace of mind.

He glanced over at the clock. It was close to midnight. After he had returned from the gift shop, Phire had awakened and they'd ordered room service. After eating they'd showered together and made love all over again before drifting off to sleep. Now he was awake and his mind couldn't help but think about the defective condom. What if she had gotten pregnant? For him that would be a game changer. Before they parted ways, he would make sure she knew that. There was no way he would allow her to marry another man if she was carrying his baby. He didn't give a royal damn about her father or whatever plans he had for her and that Ravnell guy.

The one thing Maverick had vowed years ago was that he would not be like Bart and take a child away from its mother. Co-parenting was something he didn't have a problem doing if it came to that. Of course, there was another option, one that left a bad taste in his mouth. Marriage. He could marry Phire for their child's sake. That way he could have his child with him all the time. He would have Phire with him, too. The thought made him feel something he didn't want to explore…

There had to be another option. He wasn't the marrying kind. He was certain he and Phire could work out something, and keep what would be best for their child at the forefront.

Their child…

He might be putting the cart in front of the horse. But if she wasn't right about the timing, the one thing an Outlaw knew was to always be prepared.

Phire knew the moment Maverick entered the bedroom. Although he wasn't saying anything, she knew he was watching her pack. Their two days of idyllic bliss had come to an end. She refused to look in his direction, afraid he would see the deep love she had for him in her eyes.

So instead, she thought about how much she had enjoyed the time they'd spent together. These had been the best two days and three nights she'd had in a long time. After their first night, they had gotten out of the hotel around noon, enjoyed a delicious lunch in the hotel's restaurant and gone shopping. She'd needed an outfit since he'd told her he intended to take her to dinner and dancing later that day.

Both had been fantastic. They'd gone to one of the fanciest restaurants in Dallas, the French Room. Afterward, they'd danced the night away at the Singer Nightclub. It felt good being in his arms while they danced, and more than once, he'd whispered how much he'd missed her. That had been the last thing she needed to hear when she knew their two days together were all they had.

It was way after midnight when they returned to the hotel. As soon as he'd closed the door behind them, they had quickly undressed each other and made love all through the night and most of the next day. On their last evening together, he had taken her skating.

For a while she had forgotten her troubles. It had always been that way whenever she spent time with Maverick. He had a knack for knowing what she needed. And he knew her needs weren't always in the bedroom. However, those times when they *were* in the bedroom, he could definitely deliver.

"We need to talk, Phire."

She heard the seriousness in his voice and stopped what she was doing to look at him. His tall, sexy frame leaned in the doorway. He was shirtless and his jeans were riding low on his hips. They had made love for the last time less than an hour ago and she was missing him already.

"What do we need to talk about, Maverick?"

"I know you said you doubt that you're pregnant, but if you're wrong—"

"I'm not," she interrupted.

"But if you are, that changes everything. I want you to promise me something."

She lifted an eyebrow. "What?"

"That you'll contact me and let me know."

She frowned. "You think I wouldn't, Maverick?"

"I don't want to think so, but you won't stand up to your father. The man who sounds as ruthless as they come. After being raised by such a man myself, I can see your father trying to force you into not telling me or convincing you not to have the baby."

Yes, unfortunately, she could see that, too. "If I am pregnant, Maverick, which again, chances are that I'm not, but if I am, I promise to contact you."

What Maverick had said was true. If she was pregnant, then it would change everything. He was not a man who would walk away from a child he'd conceived, regardless of whether that conception was planned or not. On the other hand, if she was pregnant and didn't follow her father's orders and marry Jaxon, that meant she might not ever see her aunt again. Knowing such a thing was possible sent a chill through her.

Maverick must have seen her tremble because he crossed the room and pulled her into his arms. "If you are pregnant with my child, Phire, everything is going to work out."

She pulled out of his arms. "How can you even think that it will? You don't know my father like I do. There are things about him that my aunt would never explain to me. The only things she would say was that whatever was done in the dark would one day come to the light. She also warned me never to cross him."

He lifted her chin so their gazes could meet. "Doesn't matter. If you are pregnant, I will claim my child and there won't be anything your father can do about it."

Maverick would claim his child…but not her? She pushed the pain of his words from her mind. Although she loved Maverick, she knew he didn't love her. She also knew he would never marry any woman. He'd told her that countless times. Phire knew about his mother and how she had betrayed his father. For that reason, he didn't see the institution of marriage as anything he wanted a part of—ever. Not even for the sake of his child. His child would have his love, his name and everything else that came with being an Outlaw. There was no doubt that he would respect her as his child's mother and they would remain friends, but that would be as far as things went between them.

"So we're in agreement, Phire. If you're pregnant you will let me know."

It was a statement and not a question, but she nodded, anyway. "Yes, Maverick, I will let you know."

Five

Maverick glanced at the calendar on his desk. It was mid-January. How long did it take a woman to find out if she was pregnant? He had come close to asking his sisters-in-law, but knew he couldn't without raising anyone's suspicions, and Google hadn't provided any answers that made sense in his situation, so he'd waited it out. He was still waiting it out.

Going through the holidays had been hard. More than once he had been tempted to call Phire or text her, but he knew he had to be patient. Since she hadn't called, did that mean she *wasn't* pregnant? What he should have done was make her promise to call him, regardless of the outcome.

He tossed several paper clips on his desk while remembering their time together in Dallas. He didn't want to think about how she might have spent the holidays or with whom. What if her father was still using manipulation to bend her to his will?

He looked up at the sound of a knock on his office door. "Come in."

Garth stuck his head in the door. "Will you be joining us for lunch? You never did say at the meeting."

Maverick quirked an eyebrow. "I don't recall anyone asking."

Garth came into the office. "I did, but you seemed preoccupied."

Maverick would admit that he had been. This was one of those rare times when all his siblings were in Alaska. Since yesterday had been Martin Luther King Jr. Day, Jess and Paige had flown home to Fairbanks on Saturday morning. Cash, Brianna and their family had done so as well. "Will my beautiful sisters-in-law be joining us?"

Garth chuckled. "No. They made plans to go shopping."

"With the kids?"

"No. Claudia volunteered to babysit, and my son's nanny will be there to assist."

"Christ, you guys trust your kids around Bart? I can see him instilling into their young minds the importance of inheriting Outlaw Freight Lines."

Garth shook his head, grinning. "I doubt Claudia will let that happen. By the way, I just got a call from Walker. He arrived in town this morning, so he's joining us as well."

Maverick nodded. Walker Rafferty had been

Garth's best friend since childhood. He and his wife, Bailey—who was a Westmoreland cousin—had twins and lived on Kodiak Island.

"So are you joining us?"

"Yes. Just tell me where."

"Loretta's."

Loretta's used to be both Jess's and Cash's favorite eating place. "Fine. I'll meet you guys there at noon."

A short while later Maverick had finished working on a document. After tossing it aside, he stood to get his coat when his cell phone rang. He recognized the ringtone. It was Phire. He couldn't pull his phone out of his pocket fast enough.

"Phire?"

"Yes, it's me."

"You have something to tell me?" He was anxious to know what she had to say.

When she didn't answer, he drew in a deep breath and slid down into his chair. "Phire?"

"I'm pregnant, Maverick. I honestly didn't think I was, even when I was late. But I just left the doctor and he verified it."

He could hear the panic in her voice. "Everything is going to be alright, Phire."

"You keep telling me that, and I keep telling you that you don't know my dad. He's still being relentless about me marrying Jaxon. He's only happy when Jaxon and I go out on dates, so I've been doing that a lot to appease him."

Dates? Knowing she and that Ravnell guy were going out—and from the sound of it pretty damn frequently—didn't sit well with Maverick. "And your father still hasn't told you where he's moved your aunt?"

"No. I can't imagine what Aunt Lois thought when I didn't come see her. Especially during the holidays. It was hard for me to pretend everything was okay when it wasn't."

Maverick picked up an ink pen on his desk and tightened his fingers around it. A part of him wished it was Phire's father's neck. Maybe he should tell her that he'd asked his cousins to check into things. He decided not to say anything yet since Quade and Cole had to wrap up a couple of important cases before they could take on his.

"I meant what I said, Phire. Your pregnancy is a game changer. I'm coming to claim what's mine. I want you to pack and be at the Austin airport tomorrow around three."

"I can't leave, Maverick."

"Why can't you?"

"I just can't. Not until I know where Aunt Lois is. If I left, Dad might retaliate and withdraw all the care he's been paying for and—"

"If he does that then I'll take over your aunt's medical expenses, Phire."

"I can't ask you to do that."

"You're not asking me, I'm volunteering."

She was quiet for a minute and then said, "I can't just take off with you, Maverick."

He frowned. Why couldn't she? Had she started falling for this Ravnell guy? "Why not?"

"Where will you take me? What will I do?"

"I'll take you wherever you want to go. Even

Paris. And you won't have to do anything. You're giving birth to an Outlaw, and from now on, I'll take care of you."

"I don't need you to take care of me, Maverick. Look, I need time to digest everything. Like I said, I just left the doctor's office and I'm sitting in my car in the parking lot. I wanted you to know because I promised I would tell you, but I won't let you run roughshod over me."

Run roughshod over her? "I'm not doing that."

"Yes, you are, and I'm tired of people telling me what to do and expecting me to obey."

"Phire..."

"I'll call you back in a few days, Maverick."

A few days? "Phire, listen. I need you to—"

Click.

He moved the phone from his ear and stared at it. Had she just hung up on him? What the hell! And what did she mean about him running roughshod over her? He was trying to remove her from that toxic environment with her father. Couldn't she see that?

Maverick placed the phone on his desk and rubbed his hand down his face when the full impact of what Phire had said hit him. They had made a baby together and he was going to be a father. *A father.* He would be the first to admit that fatherhood had never crossed his mind, but now that it was a reality, a part of him was glad about it.

He leaned back in his chair and recalled how on Christmas Day, Sloan and Leslie had announced they were expecting and how happy the two of them were about it. Sloan had done what he'd sworn to do—gotten his wife pregnant by Christmas. Neither Maverick nor Phire had been trying. In fact, everything was his fault because of that defective condom.

As soon as he'd realized what happened, he should have pulled out. Instead, his greedy ass had lost control and kept right on going, thrusting his way into another orgasm. If she hadn't gotten pregnant from the first release, then the second had probably done the trick.

His cell phone rang, and he recognized Garth's ringtone. He picked it up. "Yes, Garth?"

"We're all here at Loretta's. Have you left the office yet?"

"No, I got an important call, but I'm on my way."

"Alright."

He clicked off the phone and stood. He trusted the five men he was meeting for lunch, and more than anything he needed their advice.

Phire was fuming. Maverick had a lot of nerve. How was he going to claim the baby without claiming her, too? Filled with anger, she couldn't drive any farther, so she pulled into the parking lot of a shopping mall, parked and then turned off her car to calm down.

What had she expected when she'd called Maverick? Had she honestly assumed he would mention the word *marriage*? That he would indicate that he not only wanted their baby, but also wanted her?

Well, he hadn't. All he'd wanted was to come get her because she was carrying his baby. He hadn't even said what he intended to do with her when he got her. Would he end up being as controlling as both her father and his? He was claiming her baby without any regard for what she needed or wanted.

She didn't know how long she sat in her car before she finally pulled herself together. She placed her hand on her stomach and for the first time that day, she smiled. Just the thought that a life was growing inside of her was a bit overwhelming, but also wonderful.

Today she had even heard her baby's heartbeat. She hadn't known such a thing was possible, thinking it was too early for that. But since she'd known her conception date, the doctor had told her a heartbeat could be detected after twenty-two days. It was the most beautiful sound she'd ever heard. Maverick hadn't given her a chance to tell him about the experience before he began stating his claim. Although his attitude had infuriated her, she still felt overjoyed at the thought of the baby she and Maverick had created.

Phire wished she could be totally happy. She would be if it wasn't for her father being a ruthless and manipulating ass. Just that morning he reminded her that March was the beginning of spring, which meant she didn't have long before she and Jaxon should announce their engagement.

Their engagement!

Although her father had successfully thrown her and Jaxon together every chance he got, Jaxon still wasn't biting. And she was glad. They'd gone out together several times, and she had a feeling he was truly trying to get to know her. However, he didn't seem any more eager to get into a serious relationship with her than she was with him.

He was always a perfect gentleman. Even when he kissed her good-night it was always on the forehead. If she didn't know better, she'd think he had a girl back in Virginia. If that was true, then why was he going along with her father to court her?

She could see her and Jaxon being friends rather than lovers. Even with his good looks and charming personality, he was not anyone she could fall in love with. Her heart belonged to Maverick, even if she was annoyed with him at the moment.

She yawned, feeling sleepy. The doctor had warned her such a thing might happen. Pregnant women had a tendency to sleep a lot. He'd also given her a number of prenatal books to read. She would hide them somewhere in her room to make sure none of her father's loyal household staff saw them and reported back to him.

The only good news for her was that her father had announced at breakfast that he would be leaving to go on a business trip and would be gone for a week. Although he no longer practiced law, in order to maintain his license, there were continuing education requirements he had to fulfill. She was glad he would be leaving to take those classes in Houston. She definitely needed the break from him.

Phire started her car to head home. Chances were, Jaxon would be coming to dinner yet again tonight.

Maverick glanced around the table at the five men. They had all finished lunch and were drinking coffee and enjoying a slice of Loretta's mouthwatering peach cobbler when he decided to drop the bomb.

"I'm going to be a father."

In unison, all the forks went still, and five pairs of eyes stared at him. It was Walker who finally spoke. Maverick figured his brothers were too busy picking their jaws up off the floor. "Congratulations, Mav."

"Thank you."

"Wait a minute! How in the hell did you get a woman pregnant?" Sloan bellowed in a voice so loud Maverick was glad Loretta had given them a private room in the back. They'd been coming here since their teens and she knew whenever the Outlaw boys got together—and then add Walker to the mix—it meant loud and boisterous conversations.

Maverick had to fight back a smile, the first he'd felt like having since getting the news Phire was pregnant. "The same way you got Leslie pregnant, Sloan."

Cash raised an eyebrow. "You were trying to get a woman pregnant?"

"No. The condom was defective," Maverick said.

"Is that what she told you?" Jess asked.

"That's what I know." He then stared from one brother to the other. "Let me set something straight. The baby's mine. There is no doubt in my mind that it is because I know the night that I got Phire pregnant."

"Phire?" Sloan asked, staring hard at Maverick. "Isn't that the name of the woman you were with when you stopped speaking to me? Because I left Paris earlier than planned and you had to leave with me?"

Maverick rolled his eyes. "I don't recall that scenario."

"I do," Cash said. "I was on my way to Black Crow, Wyoming to prepare for that weekend when I'd invited all of you there with our Westmoreland cousins. I clearly remember that you called me, Maverick, whining, and saying you weren't speaking to Sloan because he'd rushed back to Alaska from Paris, cutting your time short with some woman named Phire."

Maverick frowned. There were times he wished his brothers didn't remember every single thing that concerned him. "Whatever."

"That was a good three years ago, maybe a little longer. I've never known you to stay with a woman that long. Usually, one night, no longer than a weekend, is your limit."

Maverick shrugged. "Phire is different. Her real name is Sapphire Bordella, and she's my best friend."

"You got your best friend pregnant?" Jess asked incredulously.

Maverick rolled his eyes again. "We were involved in a FWB arrangement."

"A what?" Walker asked with a confused look on his face.

"Friends-with-benefits arrangement," Cash answered before Maverick could.

"And when did this conception happen?" Sloan said. "I hope it was *after* I got Leslie pregnant because I still intend to have the first Outlaw girl in that generation."

Maverick shook his head. Sloan had let it be known, to anyone who would listen, that he wanted his first child to be a girl. "I saw Phire the weekend of Jess's wedding. That's when it happened."

"So that's why you rushed away from the wedding," Cash said, grinning. "You were hot in the crotch."

"I didn't rush from the wedding. In fact, I didn't leave until after Jess and Paige. Anyway, I got Phire pregnant that weekend. She called today. That's why I was late getting here."

"So your best friend is pregnant with your child. What are your plans, Maverick?" Garth hadn't said anything before now. Leave it to his oldest brother to get down to business by wanting to know details.

"I told her to start packing because I was coming to claim what's mine."

"You're flying to Paris to get her?"

"No, I'm flying to Austin. She was living in Paris temporarily. She's from Texas. Her family owns a ranch there."

"In Austin?" Sloan asked.

"No, it's a small town outside of Austin called Forbes. Austin is the closest airport."

"Forbes?" Garth asked, scrunching his brow. "I've heard of that town before for some reason."

"So you're flying to Texas to bring Phire to Alaska?" Walker asked.

"That was my plan but..."

Maverick paused, then Jess prompted, "But what?"

Before Maverick could answer, Garth said, "Let me guess. You never did ask what she wanted to do. You told her what you wanted her to do, mainly to start packing. And that pissed her off."

Maverick quirked an eyebrow. "Yes, I did tell her that I was coming to Texas and claim what's mine."

Four of the men—namely Garth, Cash, Sloan and Walker—shook their heads as they stared at him. "The one thing you're going to learn about pregnant women, is that you don't order them around. You have to treat them gently. More gently than normal."

"Why?" Maverick and Jess asked simultaneously.

"Because they get overly emotional. I'm finding that out for myself," Sloan answered. "It has to do with an increase of hormones or something. They cry for no reason at all. Get mad at you about any little thing, and they like eating weird stuff. Like mixing pickles with ice cream."

"And they sleep a lot," Walker added.

"And heaven forbid if they're carrying twins. When they go into labor, they'll scream at you like everything is your fault," Cash added.

When Maverick didn't say anything, Garth asked, "You told her that you were coming to Texas to claim what's yours. Exactly what is yours?"

Maverick rubbed his hand down his face. "I just told you guys. She's pregnant and the baby *is* mine."

"We get that, Maverick," Sloan said. "What Garth is trying to find out is if at any time you let this Phire woman know you also claim her, too."

"No. I figured I didn't have to tell her that. I can't claim the baby without claiming her. At least not until I figure out what else I need to do."

"Hell, I hope you're not planning to do what the old man did. Take her to court for custody of the baby after it's born," Cash said.

"I wouldn't do that."

"You sure?" Jess asked. "You look like the old

man more than any of us. I hope that doesn't mean you'll eventually start acting like him, too."

"I won't, and like I said, I won't take my child away from Phire. They are a package deal."

"Does she know that?" Garth asked. "Sounds like you didn't do a lot of talking, just a whole lot of claiming. Did you ask how she was doing? Assure her that you'd never take your child from her, like your father did to his five wives? Did you even ask if she wants to be pregnant? She does have a choice you know."

It occurred to Maverick that he hadn't taken the time to ask Phire how she was doing or how she was dealing with her father. No, he'd gotten her upset, to the point that she'd hung up on him. It was the first time she'd ever done that, and he would admit that he'd deserved it. Garth was right. Whether she wanted to be pregnant or not was her choice. He'd been too busy telling her what to do instead of asking what she wanted. Now he'd made a serious mess of things.

"Why do you have to rush off to get her?" Walker asked when no one said anything.

Maverick glanced over at Walker. "Because her father is trying to marry her off to another man."

"What! How old is Phire?" Cash asked.

"Twenty-five."

"Then she's old enough to tell her father to go to hell with that kind of nonsense," Sloan said.

"She can't," Maverick said.

"Why not?" Jess asked.

"Because he practically kidnapped her elderly aunt, who had a stroke a few years ago. It's the aunt who raised her. Her father moved her aunt from one long-term-care facility to another one, and he won't tell Phire where until after she marries the man he has chosen for her."

For the second time that day forks went still as five pairs of eyes stared at him. Finally, Garth said, "I think you need to start from the beginning, Maverick."

Phire glanced across the dinner table at Jaxon. As usual, he seemed to be hanging on to her father's every word, which put a smile on Simon Bordella's face. It also gave him an incentive to keep talking. It was obvious her father was trying desperately to get Jaxon interested in the land surrounding their ranch. Land that, she'd been told, had been left to her grandfather, passed on to her mother and subsequently to her father.

She moved her gaze back to her plate. This wasn't the first time her father had tried talking Jaxon into buying the land. However, tonight was the first time Jaxon seemed interested in doing so. She wondered why.

"So what do you think, Sapphire?"

She glanced over at Jaxon. "About what?"

"My buying all that land adjacent to this ranch."

She shrugged. "The decision is yours."

Jaxon nodded. "Do you plan to return to Paris to live?"

Before she could answer, her father quickly spoke up. "My daughter is home for good, Jaxon. In fact, just the other day she mentioned she didn't intend to leave the ranch ever again. That let me know she would want to one day marry someone interested in settling in the area."

Jaxon smiled. "Hmm, that's good to know," he said, picking up his wineglass and staring at her over the rim of it. If she didn't know any better, she'd think he was analyzing her. This wasn't the first time she'd gotten that impression.

"I have a favor to ask you, Jaxon," Simon said.

Jaxon put down his wineglass and smiled over at Simon. "And what favor is that?"

"I'm leaving Monday for Houston to take some continuing education classes, to retain my law license."

"Do you plan to begin practicing law again?"

"Heck no, but it will come in handy if I need to represent myself."

"Oh, I see," Jaxon said, and Phire figured he really did. Her father was tight with his money.

"I'll be gone for a week and there's something I need you to do."

"And what is that?" Jaxon asked.

"I know you'll be busy with your own affairs during the day, but I'm hoping in the evenings you'll find time to check on things here."

Jaxon chuckled. "Not sure what help I'll be since I know very little about ranching."

Simon waved off his words. "I'm not talking about my ranch per se. I have a capable foreman for that."

"Then what exactly are you talking about?" Jaxon asked.

"Sapphire. She will be here all alone while I'm gone. My daughter is my most precious jewel, and

I need to make sure she is taken care of. That way I won't have to worry. You could even use one of the guest rooms while I'm gone."

Phire almost choked on her bite of steak. Her father couldn't get any more accommodating than that. He was inviting Jaxon to move in here while he was gone? And that BS about her being his most precious jewel nearly made her gag.

"I appreciate the trust you've placed in me, Simon," Jaxon said, smiling.

Phire glanced at Jaxon and met his gaze. He then switched his gaze to her father, smiled and said, "Looking after Sapphire will be my pleasure."

Had she misjudged Jaxon Ravnell? Was he just as manipulative as her father? Even more cunning? Did she have a say in the matter? What if she didn't want him here?

Later that night, Phire got out of bed, unable to sleep. Crossing the room, she went to the window and looked out into the darkness. She couldn't believe the nerve of her father, inviting Jaxon to stay here while he was away. And then to outright lie to the man about her wanting to remain in the area to live. If given the chance, she would move back to Paris in a heartbeat.

Gently rubbing her stomach, Phire knew she would go back there and build a life for her and her baby. At that moment her child was the only good thing happening in her life, and she would cherish it because she and Maverick had made it together.

Maverick.

She was tempted to call him, but he might not accept her call after the way she had ended their conversation earlier that day. She had hung up on him, for Pete's sake. She'd never done anything like that to anyone in her life. Never had a reason to do so no matter how mad she'd been.

She checked her watch. There was a three-hour time difference between Texas and Alaska. By her calculations it would be around 7:00 p.m. their time. She would call him because she owed him an apology.

But before she could call, her phone rang. From the tone, she knew it was Clancy. She had asked him to snoop around to see if he could find out anything about what facility her aunt had been moved to.

"Hello, Clancy. It's four in the morning there. What are you doing up?"

"Just got back from taking the folks to the airport. They're taking a cruise out of Barcelona."

"Good for them."

"I think so, too."

"Have you turned up anything on my aunt?" she asked him.

"Not a thing. I even had Dionne asking questions, but it seems everyone who works at that long-term-care facility is keeping a tight lip. I'm sorry, Phire."

"Don't be. I appreciate you and Dionne trying to find out anything for me. How are the twins?"

"My girls are fine and growing every day. I decided they won't ever date. No guy will be good enough for them."

Phire smiled, wishing she could have had such an adoring father while growing up. "Well, give them and Dionne my love. And thanks again for trying."

"Wished we could have been more help. When are you coming home?"

She nibbled on her bottom lip. Clancy knew her father was using her aunt to force her into marrying someone. However, she hadn't told him that she was pregnant with Maverick's child. "I'm not sure yet."

"Well, I hope you won't let your father force you into marrying someone against your will, Phire. That's plain ludicrous."

Clancy let her know how his parents were doing before they finally ended the call. She barely had time to place her phone down when it rang again. She couldn't ignore the increase of her heart rate when she recognized Maverick's ringtone. Was he calling to make more demands? State more claims? She knew as her baby's father he had certain rights, but she couldn't help wondering if he would do her like his own father had done and take her child away from her.

"Hello?"

"Hello, Phire, it's me. How are you doing?"

He sounded calm and not anxious, like he had earlier. "I'm fine. In fact, I was about to call you. I should not have hung up on you earlier today. I apologize."

"I'm the one who should be apologizing. I didn't even take the time to ask how you were doing or what you wanted." He paused. "Do you want to be pregnant, Phire?"

His question made her automatically rub her stomach. "Doesn't matter now, does it?"

"But do you want to keep it?"

His question made her hand go still. Was he suggesting that she not have the baby? Had he changed his mind and now wanted to wipe his hands of the child they'd made together? "Why are you asking me that, Maverick? Do you not want me to keep it? Are you suggesting that I get—"

"No!" he said, before she could finish her question. "That's not what I'm suggesting, and it doesn't matter whether I want you to keep it. It's what you want to do."

"It's your baby, too, Maverick. Do you want it?"

"Yes, I want it."

She released a sigh of relief. "And I want it, too. I intend to be a good mother."

"There's no doubt in my mind that you will be. And I intend to be a good father. I don't intend to be anything like your father or mine."

"That's good to hear because Dad's on a roll. He knows he has me just where he wants me as long as I have no idea where he's taken my aunt."

"Well, just so you know, I've hired my cousins' security firm to locate your aunt's whereabouts."

"You did?"

"Yes. I refuse to have your father hold something like that over your head. And I meant what I said, Phire. I have no problem taking over the cost of your aunt's expenses."

She fought back her tears. Maverick didn't love her, but he was doing whatever he could to lighten her load. She knew why he was doing it. She was having his baby and no matter what, it was all about claiming what was his. "Dad's going out of town next week to attend an attorney seminar in Houston and he had the nerve to invite Jaxon to stay here while he's gone."

"Good, let him stay there, but that doesn't mean you have to be there, does it?"

"No, but where will I go?"

"I'd love to see you. I'm coming to Austin and will be staying with my cousins, Clint and Alyssa Westmoreland. They have a spread, the Golden Glade Ranch, that's about seventy miles outside of Austin. I'll be staying in one of their guest cottages. I'd love for you to join me. We do need to talk, Phire."

She nibbled on her bottom lip as she thought about what he'd said. She knew he was right. They did need to talk.

"Will you have a problem with getting away?"

"No. I'll tell Dad that I changed my mind about staying here while he's gone and will be flying back to Paris to check on things there. He won't like it, but at this point, I don't care. I don't like the idea of him inviting Jaxon to stay here without asking how I felt about it first."

"I don't like it, either, and I have a plan to outsmart him."

That sounded pretty good to her. "Okay, Maverick, what's your plan?"

Six

"You think I don't know what you're doing?" Simon said, glaring at Phire across the breakfast table.

She looked up from her meal. "And just what am I doing? I'm merely going back home to check on things."

His glare deepened. "You're deliberately defying me, and it won't work, Sapphire. In the end I will get just what I want. Paris is no longer your home. This is. And there's nothing for you to check on there. If you think you can go snooping at that long-term-care facility for answers as to your aunt's whereabouts, don't waste your time. They have my orders not to tell you anything."

Phire had discovered that fact when she'd called the facility last month, hoping there was something they could tell her. Even the nurse who'd taken care of her aunt, whom she'd gotten to know, refused to talk to her.

"Look, Dad, you're not the only one who can spring a surprise on someone. You had no business inviting Jaxon to stay here while you're gone."

"I don't see why not. He's going to be your husband eventually. It's obvious the man is quite smitten with you and if you were to add enough pressure, I'd have that spring wedding."

She glared over at her father. "I won't be rushed into anything."

"Well, remember what I said. I won't tell you the whereabouts of your aunt until *after* you're married," he said, standing. He angrily threw his napkin on the table before storming out of the room.

Phire continued eating, refusing to let him ruin her day. She glanced around and saw several of the house staff eyeing her suspiciously. She figured her father had told them to keep an eye on her and report everything she did back to him. She was grateful her pregnancy wasn't causing her to have morning sickness. If anything, she was eating more.

A short while later she was looking through her closet to pack. She and Maverick had decided that there was no need to wait until after her father left for Houston on Monday to put their plan into motion. In fact, Maverick thought it would be better to do it before he left since he'd probably have her watched.

The one thing she did constantly was make sure her phone was with her at all times. She wouldn't put it past her father to have a member of his household staff check for messages to pass on to him. The young woman who came in to straighten her room, Massie, was friendly enough, but Phire had a feeling she couldn't be trusted.

As she began choosing what outfits she would take with her, she felt happy at the thought that not only would she be seeing Maverick, but she would also be spending an entire week with him. He'd given her instructions about how they would pull things off and she was ready. Just in case her father decided to check, Maverick was purchasing a ticket to Paris in her name with a flight leaving Saturday morning. That was just part of the plan.

She turned at the knock at her door. "Come in."

It was Massie. "Mr. Bordella wanted to let you know that Mr. Ravnell will be joining the two of you for dinner. You should look extra nice tonight."

"Did he say why?"

"I believe Mr. Ravnell is bringing a business associate."

Whatever. "Thanks for the message, Massie."

Phire frowned when the woman closed the door. She couldn't wait to leave on Saturday.

"Thanks for letting me know, Clint. I'll see you back at the ranch."

Maverick clicked off the phone. He'd figured Phire's father would doubt that she was leaving for Paris. As a favor, his cousin Clint Westmoreland, a Texas Ranger turned rancher, had begun tailing Phire the moment she'd entered the terminal. He'd recognized her from a photo Maverick had shown him last night.

Clint's phone call to Maverick was to let him know that he'd picked up on two other tails as well. Did Simon Bordella figure it would take two men to follow his daughter? According to Clint, the two men had ended their tail once she'd gone through the TSA security gate for Paris.

Little did they know, the Outlaws had TSA connections, thanks to an old former-marine friend of Garth's, Ollie Linton, who'd recently been promoted to regional director of Transportation Security Administration in the southwest region of the country. Ollie was instrumental in making sure Maverick's plan worked on this end. Now it was time for Maverick to do his part.

He walked through the airport terminal, ignoring the interested looks of women he passed. The only woman he wanted to see was Phire. He glanced at his watch as he continued toward the area where she would be waiting for him.

Frissons of fire raced up his spine with every step he took. But then, it had always been that way. Especially those times when he took a trip to Paris. When the plane landed, just knowing they would soon be breathing the same air did something to him.

Maverick then recalled their time together in Dallas. Although he wanted to curse every time he thought of that defective condom, he'd finally accepted that what had happened was meant to be. He hadn't planned on being a father this soon, or ever, but now that he was one, he honestly didn't know of any other woman he would want to give birth to his child.

Phire had all the attributes he desired for his

baby's mother. Now he intended to do whatever was necessary to keep her out of harm's way, even if it meant dealing with her father. And he honestly didn't know what that Jaxon Ravnell guy was all about, but it didn't matter. Simon Bordella might think the man was in the picture, but Maverick had news for him.

Hopefully, it wouldn't be long before Cole and Quade discovered where Phire's aunt was being kept, and once that information was determined, he and Phire would decide what to do next.

He slowed his pace when he rounded a corner and saw her. She hadn't seen him yet, so he had a chance to slow his steps and study her. She looked beautiful, as usual, dressed in a long flowing skirt with a plaid jacket and boots. Today she was wearing her hair just how he'd liked it, flowing loosely around her shoulders.

Not for the first time, he wondered how a woman who was his best friend could cause such an abundance of desire to invade his body, in every pore and nerve. Just the thought that his child was growing inside of her had his heart racing at the wonders of nature. He'd meant what he'd told her on the phone that night before their call had ended. They would work through this because they had a child to protect.

Maverick wasn't sure what gave him away, but suddenly she turned to look in his direction, and she saw him.

Phire's breath caught the moment she saw Maverick. She blinked at first, making sure it was him since he was dressed in a way she'd never seen him before.

In Western attire. He even had a Stetson on. If she didn't know for a fact that he'd been born in Alaska, she would have sworn he was a Texan through and through, all the way down to his boots.

Her gaze drifted over him as he continued walking toward her. She liked the way he looked in his Western shirt and jeans with the shiny belt buckle around his slim waist. She felt the heightened beat of her heart the closer he got, and heat curled inside her.

When he came to a stop in front of her, she nearly melted when he flashed a smile from beneath his Stetson. "Hello, Phire."

It always did something to her whenever he said her name, but today it was doubly so. And it didn't help matters that his dark, mesmerizing eyes were drifting over her facial features like a visual caress.

"Maverick. It's good seeing you."

"Then show me how good it is, beautiful lady."

She smiled up at him. It wouldn't be the first time she and Maverick had openly displayed their affection, and she figured it wouldn't be the last. Besides, today called for it. They would be sharing more than a kiss. They would be sharing the knowledge that together they had made something special. A baby.

She moved closer and stood on tiptoe to wrap her arms around his neck. That's when he captured her lips, kissing her with all the passion she'd come to expect. Anyone seeing them would assume they were lovers who'd been separated for a long time, instead of the best friends that they were.

Phire needed this. To be held in Maverick's arms

this way and kissed thoroughly by him. It had been nearly two months since she'd seen him.

When he finally released her mouth, he smiled down at her. "Ready to go?"

Unable to speak, she nodded.

He took her hand, and they began walking. She felt protected with him. Maverick, and only Maverick, could make her feel this way. "What about my luggage?"

"It's been loaded on my plane. I told you about that friend of Garth's who's over the TSA in this region?"

"Yes."

"Well, he handled everything."

They had taken flights together before. He'd surprised her with a trip from Paris to Rome for her twenty-third birthday. However, this would be the first flight where he would be at the controls.

He'd told her he would fly his personal plane to Texas and land at his cousin Clint's airstrip. He had arrived yesterday and had called her last night to give her additional last-minute plans. She hadn't lied when she'd told her father she would he flying out of the Austin airport. But she had lied about her final destination.

When they stepped through an exit door that led to where private jets and smaller aircrafts were located, he said, "That's my plane over there. We've been cleared to fly."

She glanced over at the silver plane they were walking toward. He'd told her it was a Cessna. The name *Maverick* was written in bold black letters across the door. "It's beautiful, Maverick."

"Thanks."

Once they reached the plane, he opened the door for her, and she was impressed with how comfortable the seats in the cockpit looked. He helped her up and then walked around to get in. She watched him, still in awe at how good he looked. Just like a real cowboy.

When he got inside, he glanced over at her after she had snapped in her seat belt. "Why were you looking at me like that?"

So he had caught her staring. "I can't get over the transformation of how you look in Western attire."

He grinned. "This is usually how I dress whenever I visit my brother Cash on his ranch or my Westmoreland cousins in Denver, Montana or here. It took some getting used to, but I like the Western look."

"You should because you wear it well."

"Thanks, I'm taking that as a compliment." He leaned in and brushed a kiss across her lips.

She settled back in her seat as he began working the controls and talking to someone at the air-traffic-control tower.

"You look good and you smell good, too. How are you feeling?"

Phire smiled over at him. "Thanks, I'm feeling fine."

"No morning sickness still?"

"No morning sickness, and I'm glad. That would have been a dead giveaway to Dad that I was expecting."

Maverick nodded before turning his attention back to the controls. "Our destination is the Golden Glade Ranch. We should be there in about fifteen minutes. So get comfortable and enjoy the flight."

* * *

Maverick glanced over at Phire. She had fallen asleep the minute his plane leveled off in the sky. He then recalled what one of his brothers had told him about pregnant women napping a lot.

He'd meant what he told her about how good she looked and smelled. Even now her scent was getting to him. It always had and he figured that it always would.

She had never met anyone in his family, not even his brothers, and he looked forward to introducing her to Clint and Alyssa. He hadn't explained the full nature of their relationship to them, but they knew him well enough to know that inviting Phire to spend time with them was a good indication that she meant a lot to him. She did. Even before she'd become pregnant with his child she had meant a lot to him.

Deciding to spend time with Phire at the Golden Glade Ranch had been a good idea, and he appreciated Sloan covering for him at work. Even Cash had volunteered to take on some of his duties. Maverick might give his brothers hell most of the time, but when he needed them, they came through for him.

He knew they would be landing soon. He thought of his cousins, the triplets, Clint, Cole and Casey. Casey, the youngest and a female, lived with her husband, McKinnon Quinn, in Montana where they ran a horse-training facility.

Cole also lived in Montana with his physician wife, Patrina. Both Clint and Cole had learned to fly planes while working as Texas Rangers, so Clint said a runway on the ranch made sense. In addition to the security company Cole owned with Quade, he was also CEO of a helicopter-service company that provided transportation to the people living on the various mountains in Bozeman, Montana. One of which included Clint, Cole and Casey's father, Corey Westmoreland.

It was hard to believe it had been less than ten years ago that the Outlaws had discovered their Westmoreland cousins. Anyone around them for any period of time would swear they'd known each other all their lives. The connection had been automatic and immediate. The only person who still had a problem with it was Bart. But then, Maverick knew his father had a problem with anything he couldn't control. Except for maybe Claudia, he thought, grinning.

Maverick glanced back over at Phire and thought of the next seven days. His gaze lowered to her stomach and shivers went through him at the thought that a child—his child—was growing there. As if she felt him staring at her, she slowly opened her eyes and their gazes locked. Immediately, he felt that crackle of energy. And then he saw the blush creep into her features. It made her even more beautiful.

She straightened up in her seat and asked, "What's wrong?"

"Nothing's wrong. What makes you think there is?"

"You were staring at me."

He smiled over at her. "You were staring at me earlier, so I figured it was my turn."

"You, Maverick, the outlaw, need to keep your eyes on where you're going."

He laughed at that. “As you can see, there’s no one else around. It’s like we have the skies to ourselves.”

She looked around again and nodded. “Yes, it does look that way, doesn’t it? It’s beautiful up here. This is my first time flying in a plane this small.”

“I’m glad your first experience was with me.”

Phire glanced at him and nodded. “I am, too.” She paused. “Your cousins do know that I’m coming, right?”

“Yes.” There was no reason to tell her that Clint had watched her when she’d arrived at the airport and had reported two different men tailing her. He would share that when they knew more. He wanted her to relax while she was here and not worry about anything.

“And they don’t have a problem with you having a guest in your cottage?”

“No, and we won’t be using a cottage after all. My cousin Casey has a nice home not far from the ranch house. When she heard I was coming and had invited a special lady friend, she insisted I use her vacant place to make sure you were comfortable.”

“That was kind of her,” she said.

“Yes, it was, and I took her up on her offer.”

“Where does she live?”

“She and her family live in Montana, but she grew up on the Golden Glade. Their uncle, Sid Roberts—”

“Sid Roberts? *The* Sid Roberts?”

Maverick grinned. “Yes. I heard he was a legend in these parts.”

“He definitely was. First as a rodeo star and then as a renowned horse trainer.”

“Well, he willed all his land to his nephews and

niece—Clint, Cole and Casey. Since Casey and Cole live in Montana, they're satisfied with building homes on the property to use whenever they come to visit since all three siblings have growing families."

He paused and then added, "I didn't tell Clint and Alyssa about your condition. However, I did tell my brothers, so they are the only ones who know for now." He worked at the controls. "Clint and Alyssa are looking forward to meeting you since I've never invited a woman anywhere before, so they know you're special."

"Tell me about them," she said.

He smiled. "Clint and Alyssa used to be Texas Rangers. On one undercover assignment they had to pretend to be a couple and get married. The marriage was to have been annulled at the end of the assignment."

"It wasn't?"

"No. Someone let that bit of paperwork fall through the cracks. It was five years before they discovered they were still legally married. Unfortunately for them, a judge refused to give them a divorce until they lived together as man and wife for thirty days."

"They did?"

"Yes. Alyssa moved from Waco to spend a month with Clint on his ranch. By the time the thirty days were up, they had fallen in love and decided to make their marriage real."

"Oh, that's so romantic. Do they have any children?"

"Yes. Four. The oldest is Cain, and he's twelve. Carolyn, who was named after Clint's mother, is nine, and the twins, Collin and Colton, are seven."

She nodded. "Multiple births run in your family, don't they?"

He smiled over at her. "Yes, we have a lot of twins and several triplets. Does the idea of multiple births make you nervous?"

"Yes," she said, laughing. "But if I'm having two babies or three, it doesn't matter. I want our baby or babies."

"So do I. Now hold on because we're coming in for the landing."

Seven

Phire liked Alyssa Westmoreland right away. Her warm and friendly smile put Phire at ease, and Clint was tall, dark and handsome. He favored Maverick a lot. When she'd said that, Alyssa had laughed and told her about those strong Westmoreland genes. She couldn't wait for Phire to see the other Westmorelands and Outlaws together. It surprised Phire that Alyssa assumed it was a foregone conclusion that she would one day meet Maverick's other family members.

She was introduced to Alyssa's elderly aunt, Claudine, who was married to Chester, the man who had been Clint's cook and housekeeper for years. Chester had been a widow when he'd been smitten with Claudine when she'd flown in for the renewing of Clint and Alyssa's wedding vows. It had taken six years for Chester to win her over, and for her to move from Waco to Austin.

The older couple had built a beautiful home on a piece of Golden Glade property that Clint and Alyssa had given them as a wedding gift. It was far enough from the ranch to give them privacy and close enough for them to visit as often as they liked.

"You're going to like Casey's home," Alyssa said.

"I'm sure I will, and I appreciate you letting me spend time here with your family."

"We're glad to have you."

Alyssa's words were still on Phire's mind when they left in Maverick's rental SUV. He told her Casey's home was a few miles from Clint's, and that a lot of land surrounding the Golden Glade was used as a reserve for wild horses.

It wasn't long before Maverick brought the vehicle to a stop in front of a beautiful two-story home with a wraparound porch. "The house is gorgeous."

"Yes, it is. The door is unlocked, so go right on in while I bring in your luggage," Maverick said, opening the car door for her.

"Okay." She smiled up at him. A man wearing a Stetson did something to her every time.

Placing her purse strap on one shoulder, she strolled up the walkway and went inside. The furnishings and decor had a sturdy Western flair, and everything looked like it belonged. A stunning staircase led to another floor and she figured that's where the bedrooms were located.

She crossed the room to the window and looked out at the huge lake. Across the way she could see the roofline of another house and figured it belonged to the other triplet sibling, Cole.

"Well, what do you think?"

She turned and met Maverick's gaze. "What I see is amazing and the view of the lake is so picturesque."

"Wait until you see the canyon. Now that's a magnificent sight," Maverick said, placing her luggage in the middle of the living room. "Come on and let me show you around."

He gave her a tour of the huge eat-in kitchen and dining room, the mudroom, the laundry room and the wine cellar. He told her about his cousin's vineyard in Napa Valley, and because of it, there was never a chance of any of his relatives running out of wine. Phire then followed him upstairs, where six bedrooms were located—five on one wing and a primary suite on the other that was huge, nearly the size of the other five rooms combined.

"That was kind of your cousin to let us stay here," she said as they headed back downstairs.

His smile widened. "I would be the first to say that all my cousins are kind. When we met them a few years ago, my siblings and I were amazed at just how kind and genuine they were. They treat us like we've always been a part of the Westmoreland family, and we can't help but feel good about that."

"And you should. Being born an only child, I always envied those with a large family. I always felt alone."

He pulled her closer to his side. "You won't ever have reason to feel alone again, Phire. I'm going to make sure of it."

Maverick then leaned down and kissed her.

* * *

This was the second kiss they'd shared today. Phire doubted it would be the last, and she was looking forward to more. Maverick had the ability to kiss the panties right off a girl, which was why she usually went without wearing any whenever he spent time at her place. He'd said he liked knowing she walked around her house with no undies.

When he deepened the kiss, her hands went to his broad shoulders, loving their firmness beneath her fingers. She wasn't surprised when she felt his palms on her backside, stroking her cheeks through the material of her skirt. Maverick had a way of turning a sizzle into a scorcher.

Phire knew she had to end things before Maverick had her spread out on that bed. Or she might be the one to spread him out. Neither option could take place until they talked. She broke off the kiss, but he still was nibbling her mouth. "Maverick?"

"Mmm?"

"We need to talk." Within seconds of saying those words, she was the one taking his mouth again, running her hands over his muscled body. His hands were on her backside again, and he eased up her skirt, little by little, while he deepened the kiss.

When he had hiked her skirt to the point where his fingers were now easing between her legs, she broke off the kiss again, trying to catch her breath. "We do need to talk, Maverick."

He pulled back to look at her and his smile was so sexy it almost made her melt to the floor. "Okay, we'll talk. But just for the record, it won't take a week for us to talk, Phire."

She tilted her head and looked at him. Was he letting her know that he had sexual plans for her this week? Whatever plans he had were dependent on how their talk went. They needed to concentrate on their child and not each other.

He eased her skirt back down, and then took her hand to lead her over to the love seat. "Okay, let's talk," he said, sitting down and pulling her into his lap. She moved away to sit beside him. If they were going to do some serious talking then they needed distance.

"Tell me again how you've been feeling," he said, stroking the side of her face with his fingertips.

Trying to stay focused, she said, "Not counting sleepless nights, intense anger I feel for my dad whenever I see him and spouts of anxiety whenever I think of Aunt Lois, I'm doing fine."

Maverick frowned. "None of those things are good for you in your condition, Phire."

"That's not good for anyone in any condition, Maverick. But there's nothing I can do for now."

"Yes, there is."

"What?"

"You can marry me as soon as it can be arranged. Will you, Phire? Will you marry me?"

With those words, Maverick had just offered a commitment to a woman, a commitment he'd sworn he would never offer. But he knew this wasn't just any woman. This was Phire, his best friend. The woman who was full of sunshine and warmth on even the coldest of days. The one woman whose smile could brighten his entire world. But, more importantly, she was the woman who was pregnant with his child.

He would admit that first he'd thought claiming his child didn't mean getting full custody. Co-parenting would have suited him just fine. He was in a financial position to provide them with whatever they wanted or needed. It didn't matter to him if Phire lived in the States or in Paris, he would take care of them. And he would only be a flight away since he intended to be a part of his child's life. He trusted Phire enough to know she would never keep his child from him and he would have access to him or her whenever he wanted.

So when had thoughts about that sort of arrangement changed? When had he decided he preferred that they get married? Probably after he'd talked to her the night they'd made plans to spend this time together. The moment he had heard her voice he'd known he didn't want to live apart from her and his child. He wanted more. He wanted them to be a constant part of his life.

He studied her reaction to what he'd said. She'd stared at him without blinking. Now she was blinking a lot…as if she thought she must not have heard him correctly.

"I can't marry you, Maverick."

Her words crashed into his thoughts. They weren't what he'd wanted to hear. "And why can't you?"

She released a deep sigh. "Think about it, Maverick. We're best friends, not lovers."

He couldn't help but smile at the absurdity of that. "We're best friends who were lovers, which resulted in a pregnancy." As he said those words he couldn't forget how Jess had looked at him incredulously and asked, "You got your best friend pregnant?"

Yes, he definitely had. Now he'd just asked that same best friend to marry him. "Like I said, we're best friends, Phire. However, I will admit that thoughts of having you naked beneath me have crossed my mind more than a few times today."

She rolled her eyes. "We both enjoy sex. In fact, I want more of it now that I'm pregnant."

Maverick could tell by the look on her face that she hadn't meant to reveal that fact. Sloan had told him such a thing was possible during the early months of pregnancy. He wondered what she would do when he wasn't there. Would she turn to that Jaxon guy?

"You're not sleeping with anyone else, right?" he asked.

She frowned at him. "Anyone like who?"

"Anyone."

Her frown deepened. "I told you I haven't slept with anyone since we ended things, Maverick. I know I told you I hoped to meet someone and get serious, but I never did. And do you honestly think I would sleep with someone else knowing I was pregnant with your child? You should know me better than that, Maverick."

"I do, but I had a moment of panic when you mentioned your desire for sex had increased."

"It has, but that doesn't mean I want it from anyone else. Just you." She nibbled on her bottom lip. "So can we reinstate our FWB relationship this week?"

He stared at her. Did she honestly think after making a baby together and his proposal of marriage that they could ever go back to being friends with benefits? “I want more, Phire, and I still want you to tell me why we can’t get married.”

She didn’t say anything. Instead, she looked out the window. When she glanced back at him, she said, “It would ruin our friendship, Maverick, and I don’t ever want to lose you as my best friend.”

The moment Maverick realized Phire was serious, he took her hands in his. When he felt them shaking, he pulled her into his arms, and when he heard a sniffle, he tightened his hold. “Don’t ever think that will happen to us, Phire. We’ll be best friends for life, regardless.”

She drew away from him and swiped at her tears. “I’m sorry, Maverick. I’ve been crying a lot lately. All these extra pesky hormones.”

He pulled her back into his arms. “What have you been crying a lot about? Has the thought of being pregnant made you sad?”

She pushed back to look up at him. “No. Although we didn’t plan for this baby, it is the brightest part of my life. It’s all the other stuff that often weighs me down. I try not to think about it, but can’t help doing so.”

“And it’s all that other stuff I want to protect you from, Phire. You don’t deserve the crap your father is putting you through. It’s bad enough he won’t tell you where your aunt is, but trying to force you into marriage is crossing the line. If you’re going to marry anyone, it should be me.”

“Yes, but…”

He raised an eyebrow. “But what, Phire?”

* * *

Phire looked away again, trying to regain her composure. How could she tell him that the real reason she couldn't marry him was because everything he wanted to do for her was because of the baby? He would offer her the moon so that their baby could be protected and cared for. But he didn't love *her.* It wasn't his fault that she loved him so much and it broke her heart that he couldn't love her back.

"Our baby would have parents who didn't love each other."

"But we do love each other, Phire. We just aren't *in love* with each other. You and my baby are the most important people to me right now."

"But why do we have to get married, Maverick? Shared custody would work for us."

Maverick didn't reply, but she could see his agitation. Why? Didn't he know she was trying to make things easy for him? Why should he give up his womanizing ways because she was pregnant with his child?

Instead of commenting on what she'd said, he glanced at his watch. "Let's go for a drive."

She lifted her brow. "A drive?"

"Yes, I want to show you around the Golden Glade."

Knowing Maverick like she did, she figured he was only dropping the subject for now. There was no doubt in her mind that he would pick it up later when he thought he would have the upper hand.

Standing, she said, "Okay, a drive sounds wonderful. But I need to use the bathroom first."

When she returned a short while later, Maverick was no longer standing by the love seat, but had moved over to the window. "I'm back."

He turned around and smiled at her. "So you are. And about our earlier conversation."

"Yes?"

"I don't want you to feel like I'm rushing you into anything, Phire. Just promise me you'll think about my marriage proposal."

She nodded. "Okay, I promise I will."

"And just so you know, I'm taking a month's leave from work."

"Why?"

"To hang around to be close to you in case you might need me for anything."

There he was, being thoughtful again. "Anything like what?"

"Anything. I don't like the thought of you not sleeping at night and feeling stressed."

"It can't be helped until I find out where Dad has taken Aunt Lois, Maverick."

"And what about Jaxon Ravnell?"

If she didn't know better, she would swear Maverick sounded jealous. But she did know better. "I'm still trying to figure him out. He seems to be a nice guy, but then a part of me feels he's up to something and could be just as manipulative as Dad."

"Don't think about any of that now. I want this week to be a relaxing and peaceful one for you." Taking her hand, he said, "Come on and let me show you around the ranch."

Eight

"I can't believe how beautiful the Golden Glade is," Phire said when they returned a few hours later. Surprising her with a packed lunch that Chester and Claudine had prepared, Maverick had chosen a spot near the south ridge for them to have a picnic. All around them had been the open range, fields and meadows, and he showed her the reserves where all the wild horses ran free.

"Whoever's idea it was to build those cute out-houses in several locations on the range must have understood the needs of a pregnant woman."

Maverick grinned as he took off his Stetson and placed it on the rack by the door. "I understand it was Alyssa's idea. She designed them and had them built specifically for the men and women who work on the ranch. A lot of them spend most of their days on the range, and she wanted to not only make things convenient for them, but also nice to look at."

"They are and that was really thoughtful of her. I like her."

"And she likes you," he said, heading for the kitchen. A cold beer sounded nice about now.

"How do you know?"

"She told me." He stopped walking, turned around in time to see the huge smile on Phire's face. And those dimples he loved. His eyebrows drew together. "Why are you smiling?"

She shrugged and shoved her hands into the pockets of her skirt. "Because I am."

He recalled her telling him that she'd never had any girlfriends while growing up in Texas. Her father didn't allow her to socialize with any of their neighbors. When she moved to Paris, most of the girls in her class didn't bother to befriend her because they didn't speak English. He figured that's why she appreciated Alyssa's friendship. He couldn't wait for her to meet Charm and the other women in the Westmoreland family. There was no doubt in his mind they would like her, too.

"I think I'll take a nap now. Which guest bedroom will we be using?" she asked.

Maverick hadn't wanted to assume they would be sharing a bed again until they had a more in-depth discussion about their baby business. Evidently, she felt they had said all that needed to be said for now.

"Whichever one you want to use." It honestly

didn't matter which bedroom he slept in as long as she was in there with him.

"I like the bedroom with the window facing that huge lake," she said, walking over to the window and looking out. "That other house across the water belongs to Cole, right?"

"Yes, that's Cole's place," he said, coming to stand beside her. "He and his family come down often to visit, especially during the winter months, to escape the Montana cold. But they don't come as much as they used to since their kids are in school."

She looked up at him. "How many kids do they have?"

"Three, which includes a set of twins," he said, gently pulling her against his chest.

Her eyes widened. "More multiple births?"

He chuckled as he leaned in, still cradling her in his arms. After placing a kiss on her forehead, he said, "Yes, if only you knew how many others there are. Not sure if I mentioned that Cole's wife, Patrina, delivers babies."

Phire's eyebrows arched. "She's a midwife?"

He chuckled. "No. Patrina is an ob-gyn and has her own practice in Bozeman. You will get to meet her later this week."

"I will?"

"Yes. Clint mentioned that Cole and his family will be flying in on Saturday. He has his own plane as well. In addition to Westmoreland Security Firm, he also owns a helicopter service in Bozeman."

"He sounds like a busy man."

"That he is."

She wrapped her arms around his neck. "Thanks for lunch, Maverick. I'm one of the lucky pregnant ones—not only do I not have morning sickness, but so far there's nothing I eat that upsets my stomach. Those sandwiches were delicious."

"You'll have to tell Chester and Claudine that at dinner."

She smiled. "I will, and thanks for inviting me here. I needed to get away. Now maybe I'll sleep better at night."

He leaned in and brushed a kiss across her lips. "Hmm…don't be so sure of that."

"Why not?"

"Have you forgotten how much I enjoy middle-of-the-night sex?"

She chuckled. "No, in fact I'm counting on it. I told you about the increase in my sex drive."

"Yes, you did, and I intend to take care of that while you're here."

A smile played at her lips in a way that made him want to devour them.

"Then there's no doubt I will sleep better this week." Then after a breathy sigh, she asked, "So will you take a nap with me now?"

"Do you want me to?" he asked her.

"Yes."

Maverick swept her off her feet and into his arms, and decided he would have that beer later.

When Maverick placed Phire on the bed, she couldn't help smiling up at him. When her doctor first told her some women experienced an increase in their sex drive during the first and second trimesters of pregnancy, she'd brushed it off as one of those things that wouldn't happen to her. But it had. Erotic dreams of Maverick would wake her up at night, only because they were never fulfilled to the extent they would have been in reality.

"Are you going to take off your clothes or do you want me to do it for you?" he asked in a voice so husky it sent vibrations shooting right to her core.

If he did it, Phire doubted she would last because he liked touching her all over after discarding her clothing. She honestly doubted she could handle that right now. He stood there with his arms folded across his chest in a stance that was so sexy, she had to clench her thighs together or come from the sight of him. His gaze fixed on her as if he wanted to eat her alive.

"I'll take off mine and you take off yours, and let's see who's the fastest," she said. They had played this game before, numerous times, and she'd always finished before him. A woman might take the longest to get dressed but it was a different story when it came to undressing. Besides, when she'd worked in that boutique in Paris, the owner used to host fashion shows and she was one of the models. The one thing a model knew was how to do a wardrobe change quickly.

"Baby, you're on."

She eased up on the bed and began removing her clothes. First her blouse and bra, and then her skirt and panties. Her boots would take the longest because of the zipper.

"I'm done, Phire."

She jerked up her head, and sure enough, he was

totally naked. Her womb contracted with intense need just from the sight. "How did you finish before me?"

He chuckled as he moved toward the bed to help with her boots. "My secret."

She glanced over at his pile of clothes and when she didn't see his briefs, she turned back to him and cocked an eyebrow. "Have you gone commando on me, Maverick the outlaw?"

"You're asking too many questions, Sapphire."

"Whatever." He seldom called her *Sapphire*, but whenever he did, it sounded a lot nicer off his lips than her father's. Even the way Jaxon had said it hadn't done anything for her.

Maverick's hand began stroking her legs and she stopped thinking.

"I love your legs."

"I know." That was one of the things he always did—compliment her legs. Reaching up, she cupped his chin and gazed into his dark eyes. Her heart was racing, and she couldn't slow it down.

He eased them both back against the pillows. "I just want to hold you a minute and get to know my child, Phire."

His words touched her and when he began caressing her belly, she fell in love with him even more. Her pregnancy might not have been planned, but she so wanted this child because it was part of Maverick.

Adjusting their positions, he placed a kiss in the center of her stomach and whispered, "I am your daddy, little one, and I love you."

Phire couldn't stop the tears that sprang in her eyes.

His words were so special because he was claiming their child, not out of possessiveness but out of love. And it was love she felt and she believed her child felt it, too.

After placing several more kisses on her stomach, he pulled her into his strong arms. And when his mouth came down on her, she was ready, parting her lips on a desirous sigh. His tongue took hold of hers, moved around her mouth, possessing and claiming.

It had been nearly two months since they'd shared a bed. Two lonely months for her but being here with him now was worth the agonizing wait. All her thoughts dissolved with every stroke of his tongue.

His hands had moved back to her stomach and were gently stroking her there again. He pulled his mouth away and looked down at her. "Making love to you…the way I usually do, won't hurt the baby, will it?"

Phire knew why he was asking. Not that he was ever rough, but when it came to making love, he was always thorough and intense. Just the way she liked it. His thrusts were always hard, reaching her to the hilt, and making every cell in her body yearn in primitive hunger. She loved the feel of the solid length of him going in and out in rapid succession.

"No, nothing you do to me will hurt the baby. It's all good." Just looking at his aroused body let her know he would be alright.

"You sure?"

"Yes, I'm positive. The doctor said that whatever I was doing before I could continue doing. I can even continue horseback riding as long as I don't get risky with it."

He gave her a look that meant he would have something to say about her riding a horse, so she decided to save that discussion for another time. Especially when her gaze lowered to his chest. Unable to help herself, she ran her fingers through the curly hair. She always loved how it felt, and for her it was such a turn-on. Like she really needed something else to get her aroused.

"Maverick," she whispered.

"Yes, baby?"

"Make love to me. I need you so much."

"And I need you, too, Phire," he said, nibbling at her throat before licking around her mouth.

She couldn't help but moan, parting her lips in an invitation he didn't need. He was well aware of what his tongue did to her. His hand moved upward to her breasts, which were sensitive since she'd become pregnant. Those same breasts that could trigger an orgasm the moment his mouth touched them.

To prove her right on that account, he sucked on a nipple and a multitude of sensations swept through her, sending her body into a mind-blowing explosion. She screamed his name when an orgasm slammed into her. Before she could recover, she met another head-on as he kissed her other breast.

By the time he'd moved into position over her, she'd gotten needier. Her clit throbbed mercilessly with wanting him. After he devoured her breasts, he shifted to bury his head between her legs. Maverick had introduced her to oral sex and her womanly core hadn't been the same since.

He looked down at her. "How am I doing so far?"

Did he really have to ask after three orgasms? "You've yet to break a previous record," she said, "but you're off to a good start."

"I haven't even started," he said, holding tight to her gaze as his body eased into hers.

She trembled from the intimate contact and was tempted to break eye contact with him, fearful he would read what was clearly there. She loved him.

After he reached the hilt, he paused and stared down at her. She stared back. The darkening of his eyes revealed the extent of his desire and the firm set of his jaw showed the degree of his control. She could feel every inch of him, throbbing and ready. So what was he waiting on? What was on his mind?

She was about to ask when he captured her lips in a kiss that was unparalleled to any before. It was full of something deep and substantive, but for the life of her, she couldn't define just what that was. All she could do was return it and enjoy the moment.

Then he began thrusting into her, a little too easy at first, but when she lifted her hips off the mattress as an indication she wanted him to go deeper, he finally obliged. "Maverick..."

They moved together in perfect harmony. They were spontaneous combustion that had been ignited and now they were all but ready to blow. Their bodies were ablaze with desires, with wants and needs. Suddenly, her entire body fragmented into a thousand pieces, each making her stomach curl.

There was an intensity in this lovemaking that had never been there before. This was unadulterated, unyielding, relentless passion.

She screamed out his name at the same time he threw back his head and hollered hers. Phire knew she couldn't fall more madly in love with someone she already loved, but if such a thing was possible, it had happened to her.

"Ah, baby, you just don't know what you do to me, Phire," Maverick whispered against the side of her neck after easing off and taking her into his arms.

"Probably the same thing you do to me." With Maverick, she knew how it felt to be all woman because he was all man. "You satisfied its mama, so our baby is smiling."

He touched her chin with his finger, and every nerve ending within her sizzled. It was as if she hadn't experienced four orgasms over the last hour. "That's good to know because its old man is smiling, too," he said, doing just that.

Neither of them said anything for a minute. Maverick just looked at her. She knew that hot look. It was the kind that drew her in and made her feel desired. Warmth returned to the area between her legs, slowly seeping into her very core. He wanted her again and she wanted him again, too.

As if Maverick felt her heat, he leaned in and captured her mouth.

Nine

Phire glanced around the dinner table. Seeing the faces of Maverick, and Clint and Alyssa's family, was a lot more appealing than sitting across the dinner table from her father. Jaxon's company wasn't so bad, except those times her father all but threw her at the man.

"Phire, I understand your father has a ranch as well."

Alyssa's comment made Phire look across the table and smile. As she'd told Maverick, she really liked Alyssa. In addition to being friendly, Alyssa was kind. Phire thought she looked gorgeous no matter what time of day it was, and she certainly didn't look like she had given birth to four children. Four very active children. Another thing Phire noted was that Alyssa was very much loved by her husband. That was obvious by the way the couple interacted with each other.

Phire and Maverick had arrived for dinner early, and the moment Clint entered the house, after being out on the range most of the day, he'd gone straight to his wife and given her a huge kiss. Regardless of the fact they had an audience.

"Yes, it's on the east side of Austin, on the outskirts of Forbes."

"Has it been in your family long?" Clint asked her.

"I understand my maternal grandfather inherited the land from a client. The old man died without any family and willed it to my grandfather, who was his attorney at the time."

"That's sad that the man died without any family," Maverick said.

Phire realized this was the first time she'd ever shared that bit of information with him, mainly because she never liked talking about her home in Texas. The ranch had seemed less like her home the longer she'd lived in Paris.

"Yes, it was. But it stayed in our family. My father was a young attorney who worked for my grandfather. I'm told my mother had left home to attend an all-girls college in Atlanta. When she came home after graduating, she and my father met, fell in love, and the rest is history."

For the life of her it was hard to believe her father could fall in love with anyone but himself. Phire might have been young when her mother died, but she never remembered seeing her parents act as affectionately with each other as Clint and Alyssa did in front of their kids.

The conversation then shifted from her to Alyssa, who talked about her job as a freelance website designer. "I love what I do and have a nice clientele. I work around Clint's and the kids' school schedules."

Clint then explained how he'd ended his career as a Texas Ranger to run the ranch full-time, and how he and his siblings started the Sid Roberts Foundation to save wild horses in memory of his uncle.

"Did your uncle have any children?" she asked him.

"I can answer that," Chester said.

"Only because Chester believed the woman's story," Clint added, shaking his head.

Phire was intrigued. "What story?"

Clint glanced over at Chester. "By all means share your theory with Phire, Chester."

"It's more than a theory, Clint. I totally believe Sid has a child out there. I'll never forget the day that letter came here to Sid. It was from a woman telling him that she'd given birth to his son. She stated she didn't want anything from him but felt that telling him was the right thing to do. She didn't provide a return address, so Sid had no way of finding her to corroborate her story. He did hire a private investigator, who couldn't find the woman."

Phire nodded. There had never been a question in her mind that she would tell Maverick she was pregnant. "Why are you so sure there was a child somewhere when the private investigator couldn't find anything?"

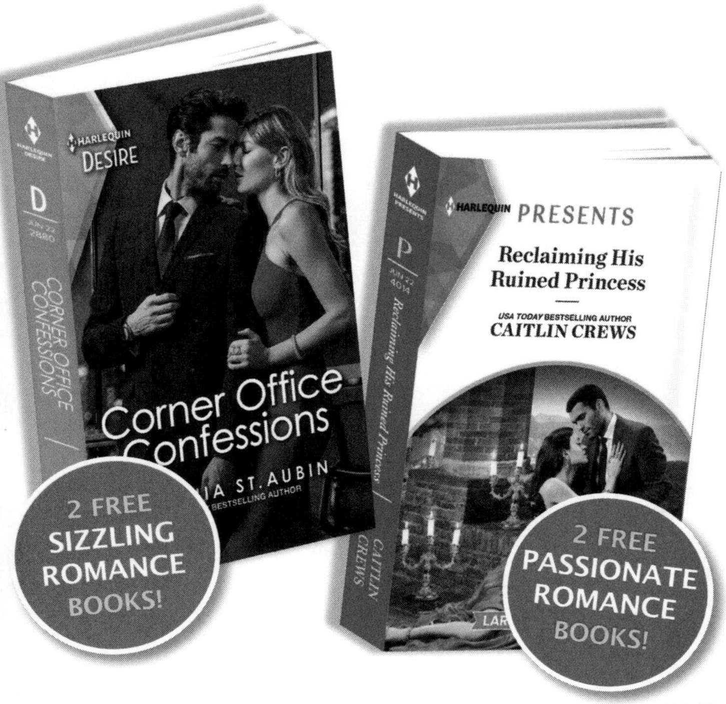

"Mainly because I never trusted the guy Sid hired as the PI."

Clint chuckled. "What Chester really means is he didn't like the guy."

"No, I never liked him. You and your siblings weren't even walking yet, and he was only coming around, every chance he got, because he was sweet on your mother. Although she never gave the man the time of day. Smart girl, that Carolyn."

Alyssa's aunt Claudine served the most delicious raisin-bread pudding that Phire had ever eaten, and it was served with the best coffee she'd ever had. More than once, her and Maverick's gazes met across the dinner table, and she would remember how their nap had turned into one bout of lovemaking after another.

After dinner Phire joined Clint and his family while the older kids told them how excited they were to see their Uncle Cole and his family who would be visiting in a week. Then Alyssa read the younger two a story. Listening to Alyssa brought back so many memories for Phire of her own mother reading stories.

"You okay, Phire?" Maverick asked her when they returned to the house later that night.

"Yes, why do you ask?"

"You didn't have a lot to say on the drive back here."

"I was just thinking about Alyssa's interaction with her children. It reminded me of my mother. I recalled her reading me bedtime stories. She was a good mother." She paused. "The best thing Dad did was to send me away to Aunt Lois after Mom died. My aunt took good care of me and all I want to do is take good care of her. But because of Dad's manipulations I feel so helpless in doing that, Maverick."

He pulled her into his arms. "I told you I hired my cousins to find your aunt. We will beat your dad at this game he's playing."

We... She hadn't wanted Maverick to take on her problems, but a part of her was glad he cared enough to do so. She knew his main concern was the baby. He didn't want her to get upset because of her condition. "And you honestly think they will be able to find her?"

"If anyone can, they will. They have a great team working for them."

His words gave her hope. "Thanks, Maverick." She pushed back and looked up at him. "So what are our plans tomorrow? I hope it includes horseback riding."

She saw his concerned look. "Trust me, Maverick. I can ride a horse as long as I'm careful. That's one of the first things I asked the doctor. I knew Dad would become suspicious if I stopped riding Salem every morning."

"Salem?"

"The Arabian horse my mother gave me for my twelfth birthday. It was the last gift I got from her. He was just a foal then, and I ride him every day when I'm home. So will you take me riding tomorrow?"

"If you promise to be extra careful."

"I promise."

He smiled down at her. "Okay then, we'll go horseback riding."

"I'm ready."

Maverick turned around and his breath caught. Phire had stepped onto the porch looking like a bona fide cowgirl. Since she'd worked in a boutique while living in Paris, he'd seen her in a number of sexy outfits. He'd even seen her in jeans. However, this was the first time he'd seen her in total Western attire. In addition to the Western shirt and jeans, she was also wearing a denim jacket with fringes, cowboy boots and a cowgirl hat that sat prettily atop her head.

"Is anything wrong, Maverick?"

He blinked, realizing he'd been staring. "No, nothing's wrong. You look fantastic."

"Thanks. Whenever, I dress like this around Dad, he claims I don't look enough like a lady to suit him. He prefers seeing me in dresses."

To be honest, Maverick preferred seeing her in nothing at all. He was liable to get aroused all over again just from thinking about their lovemaking after they'd gone to bed last night. They hadn't been able to get enough of each other. "Well, I think you look gorgeous and sexy. Does it matter what your old man thinks?"

She shook her head. "Nope. Not this week, anyway."

Maverick knew that if he had his way, it would never matter. "Here are the horses. Clint brought them over earlier."

She came down off the porch. "They're beautiful," she said. "Which one will I be riding?"

He handed her the reins. "This one. Her name is Buttercup, and she's Alyssa's daughter's horse."

"She's a big horse for a nine-year-old-girl," Phire said, scratching the animal's head and then patting her coat. "And she's beautiful." She then gazed at the horse and said in a calm, low-pitched voice, "Hello, Buttercup. I promise to treat you well."

Phire seemed to have a way with horses, which meant she was used to them. Although he'd known how to ride, he'd never done as much of it until he'd become a partner in Cash's dude ranch.

"Ready?" he asked Phire.

"Yes, I'm ready."

He helped her up on her horse and then mounted his. "In addition to new territory, we'll cover some of the same areas we covered yesterday by SUV. However, today we get to go through trails and paths that a car can't take us."

They rode at a slow pace while he told her about his brother's dude ranch in Wyoming. He then told her more about his Westmoreland cousins and how his father still refused to accept them as family. After they'd ridden a while, he said, "Let's dismount over there. I want to show you something that I didn't yesterday."

"Okay."

They brought the horses to a stop near several trees. He got down first, and after making sure they had tied the reins of both horses to a tree, he assisted her. When their bodies touched it was as if they hadn't made love most of yesterday and last night. Intense fire ignited in his loins, rushing through every part of him. He looked at her mouth and wanted to taste her lips, right then and there, beneath the Texas sky. Phire was like an aphrodisiac. The more he got, the more he wanted.

He saw the way her lips trembled and knew she wanted this kiss as much as he did. He decided to put them both out of their misery. He leaned in and took her mouth with the greed of a man who was about to have his last kiss, or the first one after months of going without.

Either scenario painted a picture that could serve as the reason why his mouth was devouring hers. The sound of her moaning only kindled the flame as she hungrily kissed him back. Her tongue moved in sync with his, stroke for stroke.

He finally forced himself to end the kiss, otherwise he would have eased her down to the grassy ground and made love to her. That wasn't a good idea when Clint or his men could wander into this area anytime.

"Why did you stop?" she asked him in a pouty voice.

He released a deep breath and pressed his forehead to hers. "You, Sapphire Bordella, will be the death of me yet."

She leaned back and smiled up at him. "I hope not, because I need you around to help raise our child."

He didn't say anything. Was she hinting at the possibility that she would marry him, or did she have co-parenting on her mind? He tightened his lips, otherwise he would be tempted to ask her. He'd told her he would not rush her into making a decision and he wouldn't. Even if he was tempted like hell to do so, he would be patient.

"Come on and let me show you something that's pretty remarkable," he said, taking her hand and leading her toward an edge that looked down into a massive valley.

"Oh, my goodness," she said, and he could hear

the amazement in her voice. "You're right, Maverick. That is pretty remarkable."

That's how he'd felt when he'd first seen it. Thousands and thousands of wild horses running free. While they watched the animals, he told her more about Clint's determination to save as many of them from being slaughtered as he possibly could.

"I'm glad he's doing so," she said, leaning her shoulder up against him.

He glanced down at her. "Tired?"

"No. I just like it whenever I can touch you."

Maverick smiled at that admission. "Baby, you can touch me anytime." He tightened his arm around her.

Yesterday, while making love to Phire, he had realized something. He had fallen in love with her. Maybe he'd always loved her and was just getting around to accepting it. Either way, just like with her pregnancy, the realization that he loved her was another game changer. He would use this week to convince her to marry him. He would indulge in something he'd never done with a woman. A courtship.

"Will you be taking another nap with me later today?" she asked, breaking into his thoughts.

He smiled down at her. "Do you want me to take a nap with you again today?"

"Um, that would be nice."

Maverick thought it would be nice as well.

Ten

Phire stepped onto the porch in the early morning sunlight to drink her glass of milk. Before her pregnancy, it would have been tea or coffee, but those days were over. At least for a while.

She smiled at the thought that Maverick hadn't gotten up yet because she had worn him out. When he'd awakened her before sunrise thinking he would get a good ride off her, she had flipped him on his back and gotten a good ride off him instead.

It was hard to believe she only had two more full days to spend here with him. She definitely didn't look forward to returning to her father's ranch. But at least she would have good memories of the time spent here not just with Maverick, but with Clint, Alyssa and their family, too.

Maverick had planned something for them to do every day. There had been picnics, horseback rides and cooking lessons. She couldn't help but smile at the latter. Alyssa's Aunt Claudine had offered to teach Phire how to make several dishes that she had fallen in love with, and to her surprise, Maverick had asked to be included.

Then there were those days they just relaxed and watched television, or went swimming and hiking. He'd made sure everything was done in moderation so as not to tire her out. However, her favorite activity was nap time because they always did more than take a nap. And, of course, she enjoyed bedtime when they would make love to the point of exhaustion, and then she would sleep through the night like a baby. And he would wake her up during the predawn hours for more sexual delight.

Tonight they would accompany Clint and Alyssa to a barn dance at one of their neighbor's ranches. She was looking forward to going, even if there would probably be more square dancing than line dancing. While in Paris, she and Maverick went dancing often, and people complimented them on how well they danced together.

"So this is where you ran off to."

Phire turned at the sound of Maverick's deep voice. Her gaze immediately latched on to his bare chest and the jeans riding low on his hips before moving back to his handsome face. She was convinced that nothing looked sexier than Maverick Outlaw in the morning. But then he looked pretty darn nice at night as well.

"I didn't run off," she said, smiling. "You'd gone back to sleep and your baby needed some food."

He grinned as he walked over, placed a kiss on her lips and gently rubbed her stomach. "And what did you feed it?"

"Eggs, bacon, pancakes and milk," she said, holding up her now empty glass. "I cooked enough to share and kept them warming in the oven."

"Thanks." He glanced down at her stomach while still caressing it. "You don't look pregnant."

She laughed. "Well, for your information, I can't snap my jeans anymore, so I've gained weight."

He grinned. "Are you sure it's all baby and not those dinners we've been enjoying?"

Phire laughed. "I have been eating a lot since coming here," she said. "Chester and Claudine's meals are so delicious." And she truly meant that.

"How often will you be going in for checkups?" he asked, still gently stroking her stomach.

"Every four weeks for now."

"When is your next appointment?"

"In a couple of weeks. Why?" she asked, tilting her head to look up at him.

He met her gaze. "I'd like to go with you. Hell, I'd like to go with you to every appointment."

She patted his cheek. "That's kind of you."

"Hey," he said, grinning broadly. "I have a vested interest in our baby."

She tried not to let his words dampen her spirits. He had a vested interest in the baby, but not in the baby's mother. Although he had asked her to marry him, she knew that was for the baby's sake. She was Maverick's best friend and knew more than anyone of his plans never to fall in love and get married. That would not change just because she was pregnant with his child, and if she married him, he would eventually come to resent her for it.

"What are your plans for today?" Maverick asked, taking her away from her thoughts.

"I overheard Clint invite you to watch him break in one of his stallions today so I'll give you a break."

"You don't have to do that since I'd rather spend the day with you."

And she'd rather spend the day with him, too, but the last thing she wanted to do was get used to Maverick's presence. Next week she would be alone again to deal with her father. "Thanks, but Alyssa and I are going shopping in Austin since I didn't pack anything fancy enough to wear to the dance tonight."

"I see."

Was she mistaken or did he sound disappointed? She figured she must be mistaken.

"I'm glad that's over," Maverick said, pulling off his Stetson and wiping his forehead with the back of his hand. He was convinced he'd aged a good ten years. He and a number of Clint's ranch hands had gathered around the corral to watch Clint break in one of the meanest horses Maverick had ever seen.

Clint had told him the horse, Vicious Cycle, was an offspring of Vicious Glance, who'd been one of the most mean-spirted horses his father, Corey Westmoreland, ever owned. At least the horse had been until Clint's sister, Casey, had broken him in. Several of Clint's men had gotten hurt trying to break in Vicious Cycle, so Clint decided it was his time to try.

Maverick would admit he'd been nervous as hell

when he'd seen the horse, but it had taken a skilled horseman like Clint to show the animal who was master. "Hell, man, you had me scared. I thought I would have to tell Alyssa that you had broken every bone in your body trying to tame that beast."

Clint threw back his head and laughed. "You have so little faith in your cousin's abilities?"

Maverick grinned. "Let's just say that horse looked ready to eat any man alive who tried taming him."

Clint chuckled. "I was trained by the best."

"And now you're training your sons."

"And daughter. Like Casey, my little Carolyn is determined to learn anything her brothers do." Clint leaned against the post and eyed Maverick speculatively, then asked, "What about you? What future plans do you have for your child?"

Maverick returned the Stetson to his head and didn't say anything. He knew none of his brothers had mentioned Phire's pregnancy to anyone and he hadn't, either, so he wondered how Clint knew.

Before he could ask, Clint said, "My wife has been pregnant three times and I know the signs, Maverick. Phire might not be experiencing morning sickness but needing a nap every day and frequent bathroom breaks are sure signs as well." He chuckled. "But to be totally honest, I overheard her tell Alyssa about her condition the other night."

Maverick raised an eyebrow in surprise. Phire hadn't mentioned that she had shared their news, but he was glad she did. "My future plans for my child are to make sure it gets everything it needs and wants," he said, tilting back his hat from his forehead and looking over at Clint.

"What about your child's mother?"

He shoved his hands into the pockets of his jeans and released a ragged breath. "Same thing. I want to make sure Phire gets everything she needs and wants. I love her, Clint, and have asked her to marry me. However, she hasn't given me an answer yet."

Clint nodded. "She does know you want to marry her because you love her and not because of the baby, right?"

Maverick then rubbed his hand across his face. "I haven't told her I love her, if that's what you're asking. Phire doesn't love me and things between us are rather complicated at the moment. That's why, other than my brothers and Walker, I haven't told anyone about her condition. It has to do with her father."

Clint frowned. "What about her father?"

"He's trying to force her to marry someone else. A wealthy man he thinks he can control. That's the reason I had you watch to see if she was being tailed at the airport. And you saw that she was."

Clint's frown deepened. "Phire is allowing her father to manipulate her that way?"

Maverick released a disgusted sigh. "Not by choice." When Clint gave him a strange look, and knowing he hadn't told his cousin everything about Phire's father, he said, "I think I'd better start from the beginning."

Phire glanced at herself in the full-length mirror. She loved the purple dress she'd bought while out shopping with Alyssa. It wasn't too fancy, and it had a definite Western flair, especially with her cowhide boots. It was short with an inch of lacy hem. When worn with the matching lace jacket, the entire ensemble had a layered look.

She liked how it fit loosely at the waist because, regardless of whether Maverick could tell or not, her stomach was a little pudgy. Pretty soon she would be showing and even if her father didn't notice, his loyal staff would. She had to tell him and deal with what she knew would come.

"You're wearing my favorite color and you look absolutely gorgeous."

She turned from the mirror and smiled when Maverick entered the bedroom. He had finished getting dressed before her and looked handsome in his jeans, white Western shirt and black cowhide blazer. "You look pretty dapper yourself, Maverick, the outlaw."

He threw back his head and laughed. "Thanks. I missed spending time with you today."

His words made her feel good because she'd missed spending time with him as well. But then, to let him know she understood what he really meant, she said, "The baby missed spending time with you, too."

"And my baby's mother didn't?"

She chuckled. "Of course, I did, but I know you really like hanging around me because of the baby."

He frowned. "I don't know how you could think that when I hung around you for two years when there wasn't a baby."

Yes, he had. But there hadn't been any pushback on his part when she had suggested they end things.

To change the subject, she said, "How long do you think the dance will last?"

"Not sure. Just in case you want to leave early, we're taking our wheels."

"You know the way?"

"Yes. This won't be the first barn dance that Tyler and Emma Baker have given that I've attended. They give one every year. They're a nice couple and you'll enjoy yourself."

Phire nodded. Alyssa had said the Bakers were childhood friends of Clint and his siblings. "I'm looking forward to meeting them."

Less than an hour later, Phire discovered Maverick had been right. She liked Tyler and Emma immediately. They had a huge ranch and were the closest neighbors to Clint and Alyssa. The couple had a lot of stories to share about growing up with the Westmoreland triplets. Phire found each one amusing, especially when Tyler told them how Clint and Cole tried keeping the guys away from Casey.

There was a lot of food and Phire was convinced the barbecue spareribs, cooked on an open pit, were the best she'd ever eaten. To her surprise, the dancing wasn't what she'd thought. There had been no square dancing, but line dancing and regular dancing. Tyler and Emma said they might be ranchers, but both had left home to attend college at a university in New York. They admitted the four years away from Texas had been fun as well as a culture shock. Although they'd enjoyed it, ranching had been their blood, and they'd returned home after college ready to get married and take over Tyler's parents' cattle ranch when the older couple retired to Florida.

Phire enjoyed dancing with Maverick. Although he was tall and muscular, he had smooth moves. The moment they'd entered the party, all the feminine attention was drawn to him. Obviously, he knew some of the women since they called him by name. But then, she couldn't blame them for thinking he was eye candy personified. Hadn't she been mesmerized by him the moment he'd walked into DuRands that night in Paris?

Tonight, dressed in Western attire, he looked like a dangerous and sexy outlaw. She could imagine him living back in the 1800s, a card shark and woman-getter. They would gravitate to him in droves, and he would have his pick. Even tonight he could have done that very thing.

Those women bold enough to approach him, as if she was not standing by his side, were introduced to her by Maverick. He called her his best friend. A number of them gave her a side-glance, as if they didn't believe it. Then there were those who had assumed that meant they could flirt shamelessly with him right in front of her. One such woman, Kim, had been so sickening that Phire excused herself to grab a cup of punch and left Maverick to the woman, since it was apparent Kim intended to keep his attention any way she could.

"You okay?" Alyssa came to stand beside her.

Forcing a smile, Phire said, "Yes, I'm fine. The party is fun, and I enjoyed dancing."

"And you do it very well. You and Maverick look good together."

"Thanks." Phire glanced over at Maverick, who

was still engaged in conversation with Kim. "And now he and Kim look good together."

Alyssa rolled her eyes. "Don't worry about Kim. Maverick is a smarter man than that. Kim has a reputation around these parts."

Phire figured that might be true, but Kim was definitely working hard for his total attention. The only good thing was that she wasn't getting it. Maverick would stare over at Phire every so often as if to make sure he still had her within his radar. Why? Wasn't Kim enough? But then, deep down she knew why. She had something he wanted. His baby.

That was why he had suggested they spend time together while he was visiting his relatives on the Golden Glade. If she hadn't called and told him she was pregnant, he would have had no reason for wanting to see her. Things would be just like they'd been for the last year, when they hadn't had any contact with each other. Okay, she would admit he'd reached out to her a number of times, but she hadn't returned his calls. He hadn't known the reason she hadn't done so was because she'd been trying to protect her heart.

At that moment the band struck up a slow number and Clint, who'd been across the room talking with a group of men, made his way to Alyssa and pulled her toward the dance floor. Phire didn't want to see Maverick doing likewise with Kim.

"Dance with me." It was Maverick's husky voice, close to her ear, and she felt his masculine arm around her waist.

She was about to tell him that she didn't want to

dance with him, but the last thing she wanted was for him to know how jealous she'd been of Kim.

"Sure."

He led her to the dance floor and something came over her. A bond between them that Kim couldn't take away. This was the first slow song tonight and she was the one he was dancing with. Not Kim or any of the others, but her.

Knowing that calmed her somewhat. But still, she asked, "Where's Kim? For a minute I thought she was going to dominate your time all night."

"Well, you thought wrong. I'd tolerated her for as long as I could."

"Yeah, you really looked like you were in pain," she said smartly, and then wished she hadn't when he slowed his steps and looked down at her.

"You were the one who left me with her, Phire. Why did you do that?"

"I figured you might want to spend some time alone with her."

He snorted and drew her tighter into his arms. "That's bullshit and you know it."

Maybe she did, Phire thought. But she felt jealous, anyway. Kim was pretty and could stay looking pretty nine months from now. Phire, on the other hand, would began to resemble a whale.

When the dance ended and another slow song followed, she and Maverick remained on the dance floor. Since he didn't seem to care what message that was sending out to anyone watching them—namely Kim and those other women—she decided not to care, either.

She loved him so much, and at this moment she

wanted to tune out everything and just concentrate on this—being held by him and knowing from the feel of his aroused body that she was the woman he wanted.

For now.

Would that ever be enough for her? The desire and not the love? Even if she would be the mother of his child?

"Are you ready to leave, Phire?"

She raised her head off his chest and looked up into dark, aroused eyes. The music had stopped, and people were returning to the dance floor for a line dance. She nodded.

He walked her to the car and opened the door. He then leaned in and fastened her seat belt. "Thanks, Maverick."

"For you, anytime." He brushed a kiss across her lips. Straightening, he closed the door and she watched him walk around to get into the driver's side.

Phire tried to push to the back of her mind that she wanted things from life that Maverick didn't want. Just because she was having his baby wouldn't make him want those things any more than he had before. But he did want their baby. The thought that she was the woman who would be having his child should have given her comfort. But more than anything, she also wished she was the woman who had his heart.

He had asked her to marry him, but she knew she couldn't. It wouldn't be long before he discovered what she knew. The baby was not enough to hold a marriage together.

She deserved more and so did he.

Eleven

"Are you okay, Phire?" Maverick asked, glancing over at her when they pulled into the yard and brought the SUV to a stop.

She turned toward him. "Yes, why do you ask?"

"You haven't said anything since we left the Bakers' ranch."

She shrugged and looked away, out of the vehicle's window. "I guess you'll be glad to see me leave so you can hook up with Kim."

Maverick frowned, wondering what Phire was talking about. "Why are we even discussing her, Phire?"

"Because she wants you and I could tell she intends to have you."

"And you believe that's what will happen?"

"Why not? I don't have any dibs on you."

He wondered if Phire realized she sounded jealous. That was surprising to him since she wasn't the type. Besides, she had no reason to be jealous of another woman when he loved her but she didn't love him.

"Did you want to sleep with her tonight, Maverick?"

What the hell! "What kind of question is that for you to ask me, Phire?"

She turned to glare back at him. "A logical one. Earlier this week you asked me to marry you for the baby's sake. Did you not?"

He frowned. He didn't recall his marriage proposal mentioning anything about the baby. "I asked you to marry me, yes."

"Well, after tonight there's no way that I can."

Maverick shook his head, thinking he'd clearly missed something here. "And just what happened tonight to make you reach that conclusion?"

"I'm your best friend, Maverick. I, of all people, know how much you like women. We ended things almost a year ago and I'm sure you went back to your old womanizing ways. It won't be fair for you to give that up just because I'm pregnant and you think marrying me is the right thing to do."

His frown deepened. What made her assume she knew what he thought? Well, it was time he told her what he *really* thought. "I'm beginning to suspect the only reason you don't want to marry me is because of that Ravnell guy."

"What about Jaxon?"

"Maybe he's holding more of your interest that you're letting on."

She released a disgusted sigh. "How can you even think such a thing?"

"I can think it because you're trying to come up with some BS as to why we shouldn't get married," he said, trying to keep the anger from his voice.

"BS? The reason I gave you should be sufficient."

"Well, it's not."

"Then, that's your problem and not mine." She flung open the vehicle door and got out. He stared out the car window and watched as she walked to the house. He wondered if she realized he had the key, and she wouldn't be able to get inside without him.

He knew the exact moment she realized it, when she stopped in front of the door, looked over her shoulder and glared at him. "Well, are you coming?"

He had a good mind to say he wasn't coming, that he was going back to the party to spend time with Kim. For her to even think such a thing must mean she was having one of those pregnancy-related, emotional moments that Sloan had warned him about.

Deciding not to piss her off any more than he already had, he kept quiet as he got out of the vehicle and walked up the steps. She moved out of his way when he reached the door, and the moment he opened it, she entered and headed straight up the stairs for the bedroom.

"I think we need to talk, Phire."

"I don't want to talk to you, Maverick," she said over her shoulder as she continued up the stairs. Moments later, he heard the bedroom door slamming shut.

Maverick rubbed a hand down his face, feeling frustration seep into his every pore. After grabbing a beer out of the refrigerator, he sat on the back porch. Gazing out at the lake, he wondered how a night that had started out so promising could end up going all wrong.

After his talk with Clint earlier that day, he had felt better about the situation with Phire and had even considered telling her how he felt about her. But tonight, she'd pretty much made it clear that they shouldn't get married because there was nothing between them other than the baby.

Hell, she could speak for herself because there was love on his end, even if there wasn't on hers. Maybe he could deal with a partly loveless marriage because he had enough love for the both of them.

"Maverick?"

He turned when he heard the sound of Phire's voice. He'd been so absorbed in his thoughts that he hadn't heard her open the back door. But there she was, and the moonlight highlighted her beauty. "Yes?"

"I only have one more full day here, and I don't want to spend it with us mad at each other."

He heard the break in her voice and knew he didn't want that, either. "Neither do I." He placed his beer bottle on the porch's banister, then opened his arms and she quickly came to him. She held him as tight as he held her. It was as if neither of them wanted to let go.

"Make love to me, Maverick."

He preferred that they talk, but he heard the gentle plea in her voice. If making love would calm whatever storm was raging within her, then he would give her anything and everything she wanted.

Sweeping her off her feet and into his arms, he carried her back into the house.

* * *

After making love, Maverick held Phire tenderly in his arms while she slept. Their lovemaking had been so explosive, he was still feeling aftershocks. Although it had been physical, for him it had been emotional, too, because a new element had been thrown into the mix. Love.

He closed his eyes when he remembered placing her on the bed and how quickly they'd gotten out of their clothes. Afterward, she had clung to him as if he was her lifeline. It was then that he'd decided no matter what, he *would* be her lifeline. He'd never let a controlling, calculating, scheming father get in the way of anything they wanted. That's the way he'd handled Bart and he had no problem doing likewise with Simon Bordella.

The one thing her father probably wouldn't be counting on was the likes of an Outlaw standing up to him. For the sake of the woman he loved and their child she carried, he had no problem doing so. It was time to confront the BS, and he would.

"Maverick..."

He glanced down at her when she whispered his name in her sleep, smiling at the realization that, even when her mind should be at rest, it was on him. It was the same with him. He had her on his mind and dreamed about her all the time. He couldn't see that changing. Ever.

"Maverick?"

He glanced down at her and saw she was awake. "Yes, sweetheart?"

"I hate to be a bother, but these hormones are at it again. Please make love to me once more."

He stroked her cheek. "You would never be a bother, Phire. Making love to you at any time is my pleasure and I will always try to make it yours."

On Sunday, Phire couldn't believe her week with Maverick had come to an end and she was now packing to return home. It had been fun, just what she needed. Yesterday, Clint's brother Cole had arrived with his family. Just like Phire had taken to Alyssa immediately, it had been the same way with Dr. Patrina Westmoreland. The kids had been glad to see each other and had taken off to do fun activities. Cole, Clint and Maverick left to go riding on the range and that gave the three women time to spend together.

Patrina had known Phire was pregnant without her saying a word about her condition. She'd been happy to ask Patrina a number of questions and appreciated the woman's willingness to provide answers. Patrina shared that her mother, grandmother and great-grandmother had been midwives, and that although she'd been trained to follow in their footsteps, she'd decided to go to medical school to offer her patients the best of both worlds. It had been lovely to get to know both women better.

"Expect me at your father's ranch in a week, Phire."

Her head jerked up from packing to see Maverick leaning in the doorway. She was surprised by what he'd said. "What do you mean?"

"I'm coming to claim what's mine."

She rolled her eyes. "Please don't tell me we're back to that again."

Especially not after a night like Friday and a day like yesterday, she thought. After making love numerous times Friday night after the barn dance, they had slept late yesterday before getting up, showering together and preparing lunch, since it had been too late for breakfast. That's when they had joined Clint and Alyssa at the main house, where she'd met Cole and Patrina.

Knowing she would be leaving today, last night's lovemaking had practically been an all-nighter. Whatever she'd needed, Maverick had delivered.

"We never left the issue. You were mistaken about my claim only being about the baby, Phire. I'm claiming you, too."

She glared at him. "I am not an object to be claimed, Maverick. Now you're really acting like an outlaw."

Why did a smile suddenly appear on his lips? What part of what she'd said had he found amusing? She slowly drew in a deep breath when he eased away from the doorjamb and stalked toward her. She couldn't stop her gaze from traveling all over him. He didn't look at all like an Alaskan. Dressed in his Western wear, all the way down to his boots, he looked totally Texan. This wasn't the first time she'd wondered if he had Texas blood running through his veins.

He came to a stop in front of her. "I hope I'm acting like a man who cares very much for the woman who is having his baby. A woman who means a lot to me."

A woman you don't love.

She knew the best way to handle Maverick was not to be argumentative, since he was in one of his possessive moments. But still, the last thing she needed was for him to confront her father about anything, especially now.

She leaned against the bedpost. He was so sexy, just looking at him made her weak in the knees. "Maverick, promise me you won't do that."

He crossed his hands over his chest. "Only if you promise me that you won't let your father talk you into marrying someone else."

"I won't do that. I'm merely trying to play along with Dad for now." She saw some of the tension leave his features.

Maverick stroked her cheek. "I'm not trying to be difficult, Phire."

She loved the feel of his hand on her face, spreading heat all through her. "Aren't you?"

"No. I worry about you and refuse to let anything happen to you."

She nodded. "I promise to take care of myself for the baby's sake."

"Why do you center everything around the baby?"

She wondered how he could ask her that when everything *was* about the baby. "No reason."

He nodded. "Are you ready to join everyone for lunch before we leave?" he asked.

"Yes."

Maverick would be flying her back to Austin in his plane. Her father had texted her that he had returned to the ranch yesterday and that he would be the one picking her up from the airport. She wondered why. Even when she'd returned to the States from Paris, he had never bothered picking her up. She would like to think he was softening, but she knew that probably wasn't the case. However, it did make her curious.

"Phire?"

She glanced over at Maverick. "Yes?"

"You're okay?"

She drew in a deep breath, smiled and nodded. "Yes, Maverick. I'm okay."

It was much too soon, to Maverick's way of thinking, when he landed his Cessna at the Austin airport. His week with Phire was over and he wasn't ready to let her go. Especially when he knew the chaos she would be enduring. More than once during the flight he'd been tempted to fly them straight to Alaska, but there was no way to do so without her consent and she wouldn't be giving it. More than anything, he hoped his cousins' security firm could locate her aunt, and soon. Phire's happiness and peace of mind meant everything to him.

"Thanks for inviting me to the Golden Glade, Maverick, I had a great time. The Westmorelands are awesome. I enjoyed their company."

He tilted back his Stetson and gazed over at her. He was in no hurry for them to get out of the plane. "What about me? Didn't you enjoy my company as well?"

She gave him a cheeky grin, the kind he always adored. "I always do. You, Maverick, the outlaw, are something else." She leaned in and whispered,

"You weren't even bothered with the increase in my sex drive."

He couldn't help but chuckle. "Whatever you want, I will deliver. Always have and I always will. And while your mouth is so close to mine, at least I can claim this for now."

"Yes," she said, inching her lips even closer. "I have no problem with the outlaw's claim there."

"Good." Maverick captured her lips with his. At that moment, he needed all of her, the full Phire effect—his baby growing in her womb wasn't enough. He wanted her to feel the love even if he knew she wasn't ready to hear it.

He finally broke off the kiss and rested his forehead against hers. "I'm going to miss kissing you anytime I want. Those seven days have spoiled me."

"They have spoiled me as well, but I definitely won't complain." She rubbed her stomach and added, "Your baby enjoyed spending time with its daddy, too."

Maverick couldn't help his huge smile. That always happened whenever she spoke of their baby being his. Now if he could get his baby's mother to think of herself as being his, that would make his life complete.

"I think if we don't deplane, the airport police will wonder things about us," she said, breaking into his thoughts.

"Let them." He looked around and then frowned. "But I'm curious as to why that guy who just got out of that private plane keeps staring over here at us."

When she sucked in her breath sharply, Maverick asked, "What is it?"

Her face looked troubled. "That guy…"

"What of him?" Maverick asked, watching the man walk into the terminal and get lost among a ton of others.

"That was Jaxon. I forgot he has a private plane. He must have taken a trip when he saw I didn't intend to stay at the ranch while he was there. Do you think he saw us kissing?"

"I'm pretty sure he did," Maverick said, not really caring.

"I need to explain things to him."

Maverick frowned. "Why?"

"Because I can just imagine what he thinks. He was at dinner that night I announced to Dad I'd be flying to Paris. Now he knows I lied about that and that I'm allowing Dad to manipulate a relationship between us even though I'm kissing another man. I honestly don't know his angle in all this, but deep down I think Jaxon is nice guy."

"Since you think he's a nice guy, will you come totally clean and tell him that you're pregnant with my child? Will you tell him about what your father is doing, forcing you into a relationship with him?"

When she didn't say anything, he frowned. "That's what I thought," he said, trying to hold back both his disappointment and anger.

He then got out of the plane to walk to the other side to help her out.

Twelve

"Hello, Sapphire. How was your trip to Paris?"

Phire stopped walking and turned to the man who'd appeared by her side. In a way, she wasn't surprised, and figured he'd been waiting to intercept her right before she exited the airport.

"Jaxon," she said, pushing back windblown hair from her face. "I'm sure you know I didn't go to Paris."

"Why did you feel the need to lie? I'm sure you're well aware that your father is trying his hardest to get something going between us."

She had news for him. Her father intended to get them married. "Yes, I know that."

"Then why are you letting him when you're involved with someone else, Sapphire? I'm not the type of man to encroach on another man's territory."

"I couldn't tell you the truth and Dad doesn't even know about him."

"Why? You're too old to be sneaking around, don't you think?"

"Yes, but there's a lot about the situation you don't know, Jaxon."

"Then tell me. I think I have a right to know since your father is all but trying to dump you into my lap every chance he gets."

Phire was about to say she wasn't ready to tell him anything when a voice from behind them caught her off guard. "Well, it's good seeing the two of you together."

She watched as her father approached. She looked away as the two men shook hands. Her father didn't bother giving her a hug since he'd never done so before. "Hello, Dad."

"Sapphire."

Was she mistaken, or was that anger in his eyes behind the huge smile plastered on his face? "When did the two of you meet up?" her father asked.

"Just now," Jaxon said. "I had to take an unexpected trip home and ran in to her outside of baggage claim. I was just trying to talk her into having dinner with me tonight."

Her father beamed. "Dinner? I think that's a swell idea."

"I'm tired from my flight," she quickly said. She was in no mood to have dinner with Jaxon. He had questions, and she wasn't ready to provide any answers.

"Nonsense. You've always had a bundle of energy, Sapphire. I think the two of you should go out."

"Like I said, Dad. I'm tired," she answered more firmly.

Before her father could say anything else, Jaxon intervened. "You have my number, Sapphire. If you feel better later and change your mind about dinner, please call me." He then turned to her father. "I'll see you around, Simon." He then walked off.

She was about to ask her father where he was parked, but the anger she'd seen in his eyes earlier now covered his entire face. "This way, Sapphire," he snapped.

He was silent until he'd placed her luggage in the trunk and they were inside the car. That's when he turned to her and said, "It's obvious Jaxon is taken with you. I don't know what kind of game you're playing, but it better end here and now, Sapphire."

She lifted her chin. "I have no idea what you're talking about."

"Then let me tell you. I know for a fact that you didn't go to Paris, but hung around town because you were seen on Friday by one of my household staff out shopping in Austin with some woman. I can only figure that you refused to stay at the ranch while I was gone, knowing I had invited Jaxon. I can't believe you could be so foolish. That would have been the perfect time to seduce him."

"Seduce him? Why would I want to do that, and what father would suggest such a thing to his daughter?"

Instead of answering her, he said, "You're running out of time, Sapphire. I told you I wanted you married to Jaxon before spring. Since you're being difficult, you leave me no other choice."

Phire felt a dip in her stomach. She recognized that manipulative look in his eyes. "What do you mean?" she asked. Her throat suddenly felt so thick she could barely swallow.

"It means unless your engagement to Jaxon is announced in thirty days or less, I'll make sure you never see your aunt again. In other words, I'll make sure you never know where she is. So I suggest you call Jaxon and let him know you're feeling fine and would love to join him for dinner."

Maverick tossed his empty beer bottle into the recycling can. Leaving the kitchen, he went into the living room. Everywhere he went had Phire's scent. He missed her already, but then that's how it had always been whenever he'd left Paris to return to the Alaska. He would fondly refer to them as Phire-withdrawals. Sharing a bed with her had always been vigorous, energetic and dynamic. And now, with her increased sexual drive, those times were even more robust.

And unforgettable.

He liked being the man she wanted to take care of her needs, and he had told her that if she needed him again, he was a phone call away. As far as he was concerned, he'd always had an increased sex drive when it came to her. He recalled the many times he would intentionally rearrange his work schedule just to fly to Paris even when his family hadn't known his reasons.

Although he'd pretended otherwise, he'd known the exact situation Sloan and Cash had been referring to when they'd reminded him of getting mad at Sloan for cutting their business trip short. Maverick now figured he'd loved Phire then but hadn't known it.

Alyssa had called earlier, inviting him to dinner, but he'd turned down the invitation. The last thing he wanted tonight was company because he wasn't in the mood. He recognized the caller when his phone rang. It was Garth. He pulled his phone out of his jeans pocket. "Yes, Garth?"

"I'm calling to see how you're doing and how things are going with you and Phire Bordella."

Maverick rubbed a hand down his face. "Phire was here with me on the Golden Glade for a week, and I flew her back home today. She still hasn't told her father about us or the baby. She's afraid he'll make it impossible to visit her aunt. She still has no idea what facility he had her transferred to."

"Has Quade or Cole found out the whereabouts of her aunt yet?"

"No. Cole and his family arrived at the Golden Glade yesterday, but he can work from anywhere since they've got men out in the field. I'm hoping they find out something soon."

"Sounds like Phire's under a lot of pressure, Maverick, and that's not good in her condition. I hope you're not adding to it."

He hoped not, either. "I'm trying to be patient, Garth, but there's a side of me that wants to show up at her father's ranch and claim what's mine. Both Phire and my baby."

“Have you asked Phire to marry you yet?”

“Yes.”

“And she has agreed?” Garth asked.

“No. She thinks I only want to marry her for the baby.”

“And you don’t?”

“No. I love her, Garth.” There, he’d said it. The only other person he’d admitted that to was Clint.

“Glad you’ve finally accepted your feelings for her. I could tell.”

Maverick lifted an eyebrow. “How?”

“By your possessiveness.” Garth chuckled and then added, “I’ve never known you to claim anything or anyone. That’s a first for you.”

He would agree. It was a first.

Phire looked across the table at Jaxon. She had called him just as her father had ordered and told him she wasn’t as tired as she’d thought and would go to dinner with him. He had picked her up and taken her to one of the upscale restaurants in downtown Austin.

They had finished their meal and had just ordered dessert. He’d had wine and she’d ordered tea, something Patrina had assured her was okay to drink while pregnant.

“Are you ready to tell me what’s going on with you, Sapphire?”

She’d known he would get around to asking questions sooner or later, and to be quite honest, she still wasn’t ready to tell him anything. But she should and she would. She couldn’t pretend any longer. Besides, it wouldn't be long before her pregnancy began showing.

"What exactly do you want to know, Jaxon?"

He leaned back in his chair. "Are you seriously involved with someone else?"

Now that was a good question. She honestly didn't know how serious her involvement with Maverick was, so she would answer as best she could. "If you're asking to determine if I'm available for marriage, then the answer is no. I can't marry you or anyone."

"Is there a reason why?"

"Yes. I refuse to marry someone I don't love or who doesn't love me."

He nodded. "Fair enough, since that's my position as well. However, your father believes two people can marry without love."

"Yes, I know that's what he thinks."

Jaxon took a sip of his wine and then asked, "What about that guy I saw with you earlier today?"

"We're only friends."

"Oh, I see."

Phire could just imagine what he was thinking. Friends didn't kiss the way she and Maverick had kissed. She put down her teacup and said, "He's a friend that I've fallen in love with. He only wants friendship. I knew that and fell in love with him, anyway."

"Does he know you want more?"

"No. I knew from the beginning how he felt about serious relationships. My heart should have taken heed, but it didn't." She paused. "There's something else you should know."

"What?"

"I'm pregnant with his child."

* * *

Phire was taken back by the coldness that suddenly appeared in Jaxon's eyes. "Was it you and your father's plan to pass the child off as mine?"

"No," she said quickly. "I would never do anything like that. Dad doesn't even know that I'm pregnant."

Jaxon didn't say anything for a long moment as he studied the contents of his wineglass. He finally asked, "Does the father of your baby know?"

"Yes."

"And?"

She wondered what business it was of Jaxon's. And why she felt the need to tell him? "And he asked me to marry him."

"So you're getting married."

He'd said it as a statement and not a question. "No. I told you earlier I can't marry a man who doesn't love me. I love him, but he doesn't love me."

"And you're sure of that?"

"Yes."

He was silent for a while, then said, "Earlier today, at the airport, you said something about there being a lot about the situation involving your father that I don't know. I'd like to know what that is so I can deal with it and him. Especially since there won't be the wedding between us that he's counting on happening."

Phire decided it was time she completely leveled with Jaxon. They wouldn't be getting married so she had nothing to lose. "If I don't convince you to marry me, I might never see my elderly aunt again. Dad has threatened to keep her away from me."

Jaxon frowned. "Both you and your aunt are adults, so how can he keep the two of you apart?"

Phire released a deep breath. "My aunt, who is my father's older sister, raised me after my mother died."

"In Paris?"

"Yes. She had a severe stroke three years ago and has needed long-term health care. Dad agreed to foot all of her expenses on the condition that when he was ready to find me a husband that I would let him."

"And he's ready to marry you off now? Is that it?"

"Yes, and to make sure I do what he wants, he had my aunt moved to another facility in Paris and refuses to tell me where."

Jaxon frowned. "Are you serious?"

"Yes. So now you know why Dad wants me to marry you, and you also know why I can't do it."

Thirteen

"How about a game of poker?"

Maverick glanced over at his cousin Zane Westmoreland, who had arrived from Denver to pick up one of the stud stallions from Clint's herd. Whenever the Westmorelands got together, someone always brought out a stack of cards.

They had enjoyed a delicious dinner that Claudine and Chester had prepared, and afterward, the male cousins had gathered in Clint's office to enjoy a drink. They'd listened while Zane brought them up-to-date on how everyone was doing in Westmoreland Country. Then Cole had shared the same news with Zane that he'd shared with Clint and Maverick: McKinnon and Casey were having twin boys.

Everyone was elated when, due to groundbreaking

research, a special medical procedure made it possible for McKinnon to be cured of a rare blood disease he'd inherited from his biological father. After three years of testing to make absolutely sure he couldn't pass on anything to a biological child, he'd had a reversal of his vasectomy. Within months, Casey had gotten pregnant. They had a son that they'd previously adopted, and everyone was happy for their family to expand.

There was a knock on the door, and when Clint called out for the person to enter, Alyssa stuck her head in, smiled at Maverick and said, "There's a man here to see you."

Maverick frowned. Other than his brothers and other Westmoreland cousins, no one else knew he was here. But Phire knew. Had something happened and she'd sent someone for him? Was it of such a serious nature that she hadn't been able to call?

In a somewhat nervous voice, he asked, "Did he say who he was?"

Alyssa nodded. "Yes. Jaxon Ravnell, and he's waiting in the foyer." She then closed the door.

The fear inside Maverick turned to anger. "What the hell. Why is Jaxon Ravnell here and wanting to see me?"

Hearing the anger in his voice, Cole asked, "Who's Jaxon Ravnell?"

"The man Phire's father has been trying to shove down her throat."

"Who's Phire?" Zane asked, curiously.

Maverick placed his glass of brandy on Clint's

desk as he headed for the door. "Fill him in, will you, Clint? I need to go see what Ravnell wants."

"And I think I'll go with you," Cole said, following Maverick out of the office.

Clint and Alyssa's ranch house was huge and consisted of four spacious wings that jutted off from the living room. It seemed to take forever to reach the foyer, where Alyssa said the man was waiting. The walk had given Maverick time to wonder if perhaps something *had* happened to Phire. How else would the man know where Maverick was and why he was here? The thought made Maverick increase his pace. Cole, who was just as tall as Maverick, was right beside him, keeping up with his long strides.

When Maverick reached the area where the man was standing, he asked, "Is Phire okay?"

Obviously hearing the urgency in his voice, the man quickly replied. "Yes, Sapphire is fine."

Maverick let out a relieved breath. "Then why do you want to see me?"

The man, who Maverick noticed was just as tall as him and Cole, said, "Before I explain why I'm here, I think that first I need to introduce myself." The man then extended his hand.

Maverick thought about not taking it, but then did. "I already know who you are. You're the man Simon Bordella wants Phire to marry." Maverick turned to Cole. "This is my cousin, Cole Westmoreland." The two men shook hands and Maverick could tell Cole was sizing up Ravnell as much as he was.

"Yes, I'm the man Simon wants Sapphire to marry.

However, I'm sure if you've spoken to Phire recently then you know that won't be happening. Not that there was ever a chance of it happening, anyway. Unbeknownst to Bordella, there's a reason I came to Texas and sought him out, and it has to do with you, Maverick Outlaw."

Maverick frowned. "Me?"

"Yes, you and the other Outlaws. Namely, your brothers, sister, and your father."

Maverick's frown deepened. "What the hell are you talking about? What does Phire's father have to do with the Outlaws?"

The sound of footsteps behind Maverick alerted him that Clint and Zane were now in the foyer as well.

"I'll be glad to explain things to everyone," Jaxon said, acknowledging the other two men and shaking hands with them. "However, I think it's time to tell you who I really am."

Maverick lifted an eyebrow. "Okay then, who are you?" Cole, Clint and Zane had come to stand by his side.

The man didn't seem bothered facing off with four men who matched him in height and build. "Like I said earlier, I am Jaxon Ravnell. But what I didn't say was that I am your cousin."

"Cousin?" four male voices asked simultaneously.

Jaxon Ravnell nodded. "Yes, cousin."

Clint then said, "I think we need to continue this conversation in my office."

"Are you claiming to be a Westmoreland?" Zane asked after everyone had settled in chairs around

Clint's desk. An assortment of whiskeys were in decanters, and everyone was invited to help themselves.

"No, I'm not related to the Westmorelands," Jaxon replied.

"Then how are you my cousin?" Maverick asked.

"You're connected to the Westmorelands through Raphel Westmoreland. You and I are related through Clarice Riggins, the woman who gave birth to Raphel's child and later died in a train wreck."

Although Maverick hadn't read the private investigator's full report, he recalled bits and pieces of it. "And how are you related to Clarice Riggins?" he asked Jaxon.

"My great-grandmother, Lorraine Parkinson, was her aunt. If you recall, the reason Clarice was on that train was because she was returning to Virginia. Her parents didn't accept her baby out of wedlock like she'd thought they would. She went back to be near her aunt Lorraine and try to make a life for herself and her baby in Virginia."

"I recall that Lorraine Parkinson was Clarice's mother's younger sister," Zane said. He was more familiar with the story than most since it had been his sister, Megan, who'd hired a private investigator, her now-husband, Rico Claiborne, to determine the details of what had happened to Clarice. He glanced over at Jaxon. "That means, your grandfather's biological mother was the woman who'd been Clarice's best friend at the time, Fanny Banks. He was the baby adopted by Clarice's aunt Lorraine."

"Yes that's right. His name was Elliott Parkinson.

My mother was his only child, and she married my father, Arnett Ravnell. I am their only child."

Jaxon paused, then said, "What you might not know is that Clarice's father, Tillman Riggins, regretted not accepting his only daughter and her illegitimate baby. He caught the next train out of Forbes to go after her, to bring her and the baby back home. Unfortunately, Clarice's train derailed, and he didn't make it to the hospital until after she'd died."

"And that was after she'd given her child away to the woman on the train," Cole said. "A woman by the name of Jeanette Outlaw." He had read Rico's report as well.

"Yes, but Tillman Riggins never gave up looking for the child. He hired several private investigators, but once Jeanette Outlaw discovered someone was looking for the baby, she was on the run, fearful the child would be taken away from her."

"I can see her having that emotional frame of mind," Zane added, after taking a sip of whiskey. "According to the report, the woman had lost her own baby a year before that train accident and was probably still grieving from that. Then her husband lost his life during the train derailment. She probably considered the baby Clarice had given her as a blessing and refused to give it back. Not even to its biological grandparents."

"Yes, well, Tillman never gave up," Jaxon said. "Right before my grandfather died last year, he gave me a trunk full of legal documents that Tillman wanted him to have. One such document indicated Tillman had allotted a huge sum of money in his will to continue searching for the child he claimed was his heir."

"Okay, so Clarice Riggins's father looked for her baby and never found him," Maverick said, putting down his glass to lean toward Jaxon. "What does any of that have to do with Simon Bordella?"

"According to the legal documents left with my grandfather, Tillman's trusted attorney, Wylan Nader, was given instructions to continue looking for the child even after Tillman died. Like I said, such directives were placed in the will and funds set aside to do so. And from what I can see, Wylan Nader did as Tillman requested," Jaxon said.

Jaxon took another sip of his drink before continuing. "Ten years after Tillman's death, Wylan came down with cancer. That's when he instructed a young attorney who worked in his office to continue carrying out Tillman's wishes if anything was to happen to him. I have legal documents signed by that young attorney agreeing that he would continue the search, as well as make sure the ranch was kept in good shape until the Riggins heir was found."

Maverick sat up straight and looked at Clint. Immediately, he knew they were both remembering what Phire had told them at dinner that first day she'd spent on the Golden Glade. "Simon Bordella was that young attorney. Wasn't he?" he asked.

Jaxon nodded. "Yes. Bordella was that young attorney. As soon as Wylan Nader died, Bordella ended the private investigators' search and claimed all of the Riggins wealth as his own. That included the ranch and all the land surrounding it."

"And how was he able to get away with doing that?" Zane asked.

"First, he forged a document claiming Riggins gave Nader rights to do as he saw fit with the land if his heir was never found. When Nader died, Bordella stated the land belonged to Nader's daughter. Then to make sure no one questioned what he did, he married her."

"Phire's mom?" Maverick asked.

"Yes," Jaxon said. "Tillman Riggins's trusted attorney was Phire's grandfather. And there is something else I think you need to know."

"What?" Maverick asked.

"Bordella is not Sapphire's biological father."

Maverick blinked. "And you know this how?"

"From letters that Wylan Nader wrote my grandfather. Over the years the two established a rather close friendship through frequent correspondence. Tillman was adamant about my grandfather keeping a copy of every legal document. Obviously, Wylan Nader didn't apprise Bordella that he was doing so."

Jaxon adjusted his long legs in front of him. "In one letter I read, Nader told my grandfather about his cancer and that he was prepared to die, but was concerned for his daughter. She had gotten pregnant while away at an all-girls school and he didn't intend to make the same mistake in the treatment of his daughter that Tillman had made with his. He said a young attorney in his office had agreed to marry her and be a good father to her child if Nader signed the law practice over to him when he died, free and clear."

"Good father, my ass," Maverick said through

clenched teeth. "He's nothing but controlling. I would hate to think how he treated his wife."

"Phire has never said?" Clint asked Maverick.

"No. All she said was that she didn't think they were in love." Maverick studied Jaxon. "Why didn't you level with Phire and tell her what you told me?"

"Because when I arrived in town and saw how Bordella was trying to push a marriage between me and his daughter, and then after meeting her and seeing she wasn't giving him any pushback, I assumed that maybe she was in on his scheme," Jaxon said. "I decided to keep my eyes on the both of them."

He then added, "I had her followed her first week back home from Paris. Imagine my shock when the guy following her reported to me that she left and hooked up with you, Maverick, in Dallas. I couldn't understand how she could seem agreeable to something developing between us when she was having an affair with you. I immediately suspected that Bordella had found out you were a descendant of the Riggins heir and that with her help, he was covering all bases."

"When did you discover differently?" Zane asked.

"It soon became obvious that although her father was trying to push something between us, Sapphire wasn't having it. I can tell when a woman isn't interested in a man and it became quite clear to me, even if it wasn't to her father, that she wasn't interested."

He then added, "I knew for certain when Bordella made plans to go out of town and he invited me to stay at the ranch with Sapphire unchaperoned. If she had been in on her father's plan, she would have used that week to try to seduce me. Instead, she announced that she intended to go to Paris that same week. That ruined Bordella's plans for a seduction and I could tell he wasn't happy about it. I later discovered that instead of flying off to Paris, she was spending a week here with you."

When Maverick lifted his brow, Jaxon smiled. "Like I said, I was having her followed."

"I noticed," Clint said. "Maverick suspected her father would have someone following her, so as a favor to him, I was stationed outside the airport when she arrived. I saw two men tailing her instead of one."

Jaxon nodded. "One was my man Lockley, who handles all my investigations and security. The other was a ranch hand Bordella assigned to tail her when he didn't believe her story about going to Paris."

"So now you know the truth, that Phire is an innocent victim in all of this," Maverick said.

"Yes. She told me last night that her father is using her sick aunt to make her do everything he wants her to do."

"Do you know why Bordella is desperate to marry her off to some wealthy guy?" Cole asked.

"Yes," Jaxon said, after taking a sip of whiskey. "He's strapped for money due to a bad investment. To get out of debt he wants to sell the ranch and all the land surrounding it."

"A ranch and land that doesn't even belong to him," Maverick muttered.

"Right. He has until June to pay off his debt. Maybe he's fearful if he sells it, someone will discover that he got the ranch and land illegally. I guess he assumes if I become his son-in-law that I won't ask questions if he sold the land to me."

Maverick nodded. "Do you think he's a threat to Phire?"

"I won't say he's a threat, but I can see him getting pretty pissed off if a wedding between us doesn't take place in the time frame that he needs it to. Therefore, I would advise you to keep a check on her."

"I do that, anyway," Maverick said.

When the room got quiet, Zane spoke up. "So it sounds like this Bordella is claiming land and a ranch that rightly belongs to the Riggins heir, who was your grandfather, Maverick."

Maverick nodded again. "And with my grandfather's death that makes Bart the legitimate heir."

Cole snorted. "Good luck on that one. Your father refuses to claim any connection to Raphel Westmoreland, which means he won't claim a connection to Clarice Riggins, either."

Maverick took a sip of his drink. "You're probably right, but I think it's time my brothers and I confront Dad about his refusal to acknowledge his past. Once I tell them everything, my brothers will agree with me." He glanced over at Jaxon. "I'd like you to come to Alaska to meet my brothers and tell them what you've told us."

"That's no problem," Jaxon said. "I'll have my attorneys provide copies of all the legal documents and letters." He paused. "There is something else you need to know."

"What?"

"To weed out imposters who might have pretended to be the Riggins heir, Tillman had the necessary lab work done on Clarice's body, so that if the child was ever found they could do a blood test. Now, with DNA testing, it would be easy to determine if your father is the legitimate son of the Riggins heir."

"Yes, but the key is getting my father to agree to such a test," Maverick said, frowning. "Knowing Bartram Outlaw like I do, regardless of whether or not the test will prove things, he will refuse to do it. He's just that pigheaded."

The room got silent and then Jaxon turned to Maverick. "There is another matter I need to talk to you about and it's rather private."

Maverick was about to say that anything Jaxon had to discuss with him could be said in front of his cousins, but changed his mind. Standing, he said, "I was about to leave for where I'm staying while I'm here. We can go and talk there."

Fourteen

"Massie said you wanted to see me, Dad," Phire said, entering her father's office. She had been running water for her bath when Massie had knocked on her bedroom door and said he'd wanted to see her.

He had barely exchanged a word with her during dinner after inquiring about her date with Jaxon the night before. He was anxious to see if wedding plans had been made. Obviously, he didn't think a courtship or an engagement needed to take place before a wedding.

There was no doubt in her mind that Jaxon would not set foot on her father's ranch again now that he knew the truth. So where did that leave her with getting any information on her aunt? She had spoken to

Maverick last night and he'd again given her hope that his cousins could find her aunt.

Her father finally looked up from the papers on his desk and stared at her. There was an angry expression on his features, but then that wasn't uncommon. The only time he wasn't angry was in Jaxon's presence, when he pretended the two of them had a great father-daughter relationship.

"Are you pregnant, Sapphire?"

She wondered how he knew. She didn't want to believe Jaxon had told him, but if not Jaxon, then who? "Why would you ask me something like that?"

"Because of these," he said, pulling her prenatal books out of a side drawer and tossing them on the floor in front of her. "Massie found them in your room."

Her anger flared. "She had no right to go through my things."

"Just answer the damn question," he snapped.

"I'm not answering anything."

"You will tell me what I want to know," he said, hitting his desk with his fist so hard it made Phire jump.

She saw anger in his face like she'd never seen before. "And what if I am?"

"Then for your sake, it better be Jaxon Ravnell's baby."

"It's not," she said, knowing she was affirming her pregnancy.

"Well, I don't care whose it is. You either make Jaxon believe the baby is his or get rid of it."

"What! I will do neither of those things."

"You will do what I say, Sapphire."

"No, I will not. Not even your threats about keeping me from Aunt Lois will make me," she said, her voice just as loud as his. "I refuse to let you manipulate me any further."

He came from around the desk to stand in front of her. "Who's the baby's father?" he asked. When she didn't answer, he all but screamed, "Tell me who he is."

She would not tell him anything about Maverick, but she did say something that was the truth. "A guy I met in Paris."

He stared at her for a long moment. "You're no better than your mother."

"What are you talking about?"

Instead of answering her, he went back around his desk. "I will give you time to think about which of those two choices you're going to make, Sapphire. Until you do, I forbid you to leave the ranch or have contact with anyone."

She moved to stand in front of his desk and placed her hands on her hips. "I'm twenty-five and not a child. You can't forbid me to do anything."

"You think not? Then think again. And to make sure you don't try reaching out to that girlfriend you went shopping with last week when I thought you were in Paris, I've asked Massie to confiscate your phone and—"

"You did what!" Not waiting for his answer, she rushed from the office to her bedroom to find the contents of her purse had been dumped on her bed. She heard Massie moving around in the bathroom.

Phire then remembered she had placed her phone on the bathroom vanity while running her bathwater. She walked in just as Massie was picking up her phone.

"Give me my phone," she demanded.

The woman was startled by the sound of her voice, and when she threw up her hand the phone went flying across the bathroom and landed in the tub of water. Phire quickly moved to retrieve it while Massie rushed from the room. Phire grabbed a towel, hoping the water hadn't damaged it, even though it wasn't the newest model or waterproof. When she tried using it, she saw it wouldn't work. Frustrated, she walked out of the bathroom, intending to confront her father again, when she heard the sound of her bedroom door being locked. When had an outside lock been installed on her door?

Phire quickly walked over to her bedroom window. One of the ranch hands was stationed there. She couldn't believe it. Her father was holding her hostage, just like he had threatened to do. And she couldn't call for help.

"What do you have to talk to me privately about, Jaxon?" Maverick asked as he stared at the man sitting across from him at the kitchen table.

He'd suggested they ride in the same vehicle over to where he was staying. That way he could get to know the man better. It was obvious Jaxon was doing well for himself. Maverick would even admit to checking him out on the internet when Phire had first mentioned him. However, at no time had he thought he and the man were related.

Maverick knew that Jaxon's paternal grandfather, Jasper Ravnell, had started the Ravnell Institute of Technology over sixty years ago to work on technological advances in higher learning. He'd read there was a waiting list to get a masters degree in technology management from the institute. Once in hand, most graduates were offered a six-figure job.

Jaxon's father spearheaded the business side, with Ravnell Technology, Inc., and to make sure they were getting the best of the best, over sixty percent of their employees were graduates of their institute. Both the institute and firm were located in Dumfries, Virginia. Considering the man's portfolio, no wonder Bordella wanted him for a son-in-law.

"It's about Sapphire."

Maverick frowned. "What about Phire?"

"She told me the two of you are good friends, so I thought I'd bring something to your attention."

As far as Maverick was concerned, he and Phire were more than *good friends*. "What do you need to bring to my attention?"

"Bordella found out that Phire didn't go to Paris like she claimed. She was seen in town shopping by one of his household staff, who reported it to him. The reason I know this is because, unknown to Bordella, my security firm got one of their men hired on as a ranch hand and he overheard the servants talking about it."

Maverick recalled the day Phire left the Golden Glade to go shopping with Alyssa. "When I talked to Phire last night, she said her father knew she hadn't gone to Paris but he thinks she was spending time with a girlfriend since she wasn't seen with a man." Maverick paused. "She also mentioned that she'd told you about the baby."

"Yes, she told me," Jaxon said.

"And something you said earlier isn't completely correct. Phire and I are more than friends—I want to marry her."

Jaxon took a sip of his coffee. "Yes, she told me you asked her to marry you. However, she also told me she doesn't plan to marry anyone who doesn't love her."

Maverick nodded. "I am in love with her," he said, seeing no reason not to admit it. Especially when he wanted Jaxon to know where he stood with Phire.

Jaxon put down his coffee cup. "I doubt she knows how you feel, Maverick."

Phire paced the confines of her bedroom, not believing that her father was keeping her here against her will. What in the world had come over him? Did he honestly think she would do anything he wanted after this? Not even her aunt would want her to allow him to treat her this way. That only made her wonder why he was so hell-bent on marrying her off to Jaxon. Granted, he liked manipulating people, but she had a feeling it was more than that.

She had planned to sneak into her father's office and go through his papers tonight to see if she could find anything that would tell her where her aunt was being kept. Now she could kiss that plan goodbye. Not only did he have some ranch hand stationed outside her window, but she also knew Massie was keeping the door locked.

She glanced at the clock on her nightstand. This was usually the time when she would be expecting a call from Maverick. He'd said he would call her tonight. Had he tried? Would he suspect anything when he didn't reach her? And just how long did her father intend to keep her here? She'd told Jaxon the truth, so chances were he wouldn't be coming back, and as far as her ending her pregnancy, that wouldn't be happening.

In the past, Maverick's possessiveness had teed her off. But now she would give anything for him to find a way to come claim her and his baby.

Why wasn't Phire answering her phone?

Maverick tried calling her for the third time that night. And she'd told him she kept her phone with her at all times.

He began pacing his bedroom. Okay, so Bordella wasn't Phire's biological father, but he had raised her, so Maverick wanted to believe that no matter how manipulative the man was, he wouldn't harm a hair on Phire's head.

Maverick drew in a deep breath and tried calling her again. Instead of ringing, it again went straight to voice mail. "Baby, call me and let me know you're okay."

He left the bedroom to pace the living room for a while. He jumped at the sound of his phone ringing and knew it wasn't Phire since she had a special ringtone. He quickly pulled out his phone and saw it was Jaxon. He wondered what he wanted when Jaxon had left here just a couple of hours ago.

"Yes, Jaxon?" he asked.

"I just got a call from the guy posing as a ranch hand on the Bordella ranch."

The hairs on the back of Maverick's neck stood up. He had a feeling he wasn't going to like whatever Jaxon had to tell him. "And?"

"Bordella is holding Sapphire hostage."

Maverick blinked. "What do you mean he's holding her hostage?"

"My guy didn't have all the details, but Phire has been locked in her bedroom and a guard is stationed outside her door and outside her bedroom window."

"What the hell! I'm leaving to go there right now and—"

"No, Maverick. I believe she'll be okay for tonight. I think we should come up with a plan. You might want to include your cousins on this. Start the coffee. I'm on my way."

Fifteen

The next morning Simon heard the knock on his office door and glanced up. "Come in." When he saw it was Massie, he asked, "What do you want?"

"Mr. Ravnell is here to see Miss Sapphire and he has a gentleman with him."

Simon immediately stood. He had hoped Jaxon wouldn't come around until he had talked some sense into Sapphire by showing her that he meant business. "Where are they?"

"I've seated them in the parlor."

"Good. I'll join them there in a minute. In the meantime, see to their comfort."

"Yes, sir."

It didn't take long before Simon walked into the room where the men were seated. They stood when he entered. "Jaxon," he greeted heartily with a huge smile on his face. "This is a surprise. I called you twice yesterday and when I didn't hear from you, I thought perhaps you were out of town."

"No, I was in meetings most of the day with representatives from my firm in Virginia. I'd like you to meet my cousin, who just arrived in town to visit me, Maverick Outlaw. Maverick, this is Sapphire's father, Simon Bordella." The two men shook hands.

"I want to introduce Maverick to Sapphire. Then he will understand why I am so taken with her. Is she available?"

Maverick had been observing Bordella's features and saw no sign that he'd recognized the Outlaw name. That meant the man had ended the search for the Riggins' heir without reading any of the private investigators' reports.

Another thing Maverick had noticed was just how pleased Bordella had been with Jaxon's admission of being taken with Phire. However, when Jaxon requested to see her, Maverick picked up Bordella's tension and figured Jaxon had as well.

"Ah, Sapphire isn't up yet."

Jaxon glanced at his watch. "It's almost noon. Is she ill?"

"No," Bordella said quickly. "She was up late reading, and I guess she decided to sleep in."

"Be careful of women who stay in bed late in the mornings, cuz," Maverick said, grinning over at Jaxon. "They tend to be lazy, no matter how beautiful they are."

Maverick could tell Bordella didn't like his comment because it put Phire's suitability for Jaxon into question. "My daughter is anything but lazy," the man said defensively.

"Never mind, Maverick," Jaxon said, grinning. "He has a warped sense of humor. We will visit with Sapphire another time."

"Or maybe not," Maverick said. "I need to introduce you to that woman I met on the plane. Now she was really classy—"

"I'm sure when I let Sapphire know you're here she will want to see you," Bordella interrupted. It was obvious he hadn't liked Maverick's suggestion of Jaxon meeting another woman.

Bordella gave Maverick an annoyed look, but Maverick didn't give a damn. He wasn't leaving here until he saw Phire, even if he had to tear this house apart to find her. He was still trying to control the anger he'd felt after receiving the call from his cousin Quade that morning. His men had found the whereabouts of Phire's aunt.

"Are you sure she will see us? I'd hate to inconvenience her," Jaxon said.

"No inconvenience. Just have a seat and I'll go get her." Bordella then walked off.

"I still say you need to marry a woman with more spunk," Maverick said to Jaxon, deliberately loud enough to reach Bordella's ears.

Phire glanced at her bedroom door when she heard it being unlocked. When it opened, her father was standing there wearing an anxious look. "Good. You're up and dressed already."

"What's good about it when I'm being kept here against my will?" she snapped.

Ignoring what she'd said, he closed the door and walked over to her. "Jaxon is here to see you with some relative of his. I want you to go out there and impress them both."

He'd gone off the deep end if he thought she would do any such thing. "I will not!"

"Yes, you will! I've instructed that facility where your aunt is being kept to discontinue her care when they get a call from me. You do know what that means if that happens, right?"

Yes, Phire knew, but then she remembered what Maverick had said about helping with her aunt's care. "Fine, just tell me where she is and I will begin taking care of her myself."

"Not only will I not tell you where she is, I'll remove her from Paris and you'll never find her. Maybe to some homeless shelter for ill people like her."

A pain settled around Phire's heart. "She's your sister. How can you be so cruel?"

Her father began laughing so loudly Phire thought he had lost his mind. "My sister? That's where you're wrong. Lois isn't my sister. She's my mother."

Phire's hand flew to her throat in shock. "Your mother?"

"Yes, my mother. She was raped at fourteen and gave me up for adoption. It was only after I became an attorney that I tracked her down living a good life in Paris. If she only knew the life I lived as a child in foster care… So don't you dare tell me how I should take care of her. She means nothing to me. The only reason I took care of her health needs was to use you to my advantage when the time came."

"Use me to your advantage?"

"Yes. Like I told you, Jaxon is loaded and I want him as a son-in-law. A marriage will take place between the two of you, whether you want it to or not."

"You're a ruthless man."

"I couldn't care less what you think of me. Just consider Lois and what will happen to her if you don't give me what I want. Now go out there so he can introduce you to his cousin. I have a feeling he places stock on what that jackass thinks, so you better impress the man."

"How can I pretend everything is okay and impress anyone?"

"That's for you to figure out. Just remember what's at stake. And if you give Jaxon reason to think anything is wrong, I will make that call and you won't be able to save Lois."

He looked at his watch. "I'll give you ten minutes and then I expect you to meet us in the parlor with a huge smile on your face." He glanced at her outfit, a pair of jeans and a top. "Change into a dress. One that makes you look feminine. I want him to see what a beautiful daughter I have."

Phire watched as her father walked out the door. She dropped down on the bed, thinking about what he'd said. Was he actually Aunt Lois's son? Her aunt had been raped at fourteen and had given up the child for adoption? It was obvious he held that choice against her aunt. But what would a fourteen-year-old have done with a baby?

Phire wanted to believe her father's words were lies, but she had a feeling he'd spoken the truth. Was that why her aunt had never spoken ill of her father? If what her father said was true, then her aunt was her grandmother.

Phire rubbed her forehead when she felt a headache coming on. Her father didn't know that Jaxon knew the truth. Phire was surprised he was here. And he had brought a cousin for her to meet? That didn't make sense. She was determined to give him some kind of sign that she needed his help.

Following her father's orders, she put on a dress. She combed out her hair and tried making herself look as pretty as possible. In less than the ten minutes he'd allotted, she walked out of her bedroom and headed for the parlor. The moment she entered, she came up short. Standing beside Jaxon, talking with her father, was Maverick.

What was Maverick up to? Was Jaxon in on it? How? Why? The three men turned, and she knew Maverick saw all the questions in her eyes. And she could clearly see the message in his.

I have come to claim what's mine.

It was as if he'd spoken aloud yet he hadn't moved his lips.

She moved toward Maverick and extended her hand, forcing a smile. "Hello. I'm Sapphire Bordella."

"And I'm Maverick Outlaw." He paused for a quick second. "You're right, Jaxon. She's beautiful." Maverick didn't want to let go of Phire's hand. It felt warm in his...and it was trembling. He studied her eyes and knew no matter what, he wouldn't leave here without her.

"You better watch your cousin, Jaxon, or he'll take your girl."

Maverick released Phire's hand after her father's statement. Although the older man had spoken in jest, he didn't know the half of it. Phire was already Maverick's.

Phire turned her attention away from him and gave Jaxon a smile. "Hello, Jaxon, it's good seeing you again."

"Hello, Sapphire. Your father said you slept late this morning. Are you okay?"

Her smile widened. "Yes, I'm fine. Thanks for asking."

"Then how about lunch?" Maverick suggested. "I'd like to get to know you better, Sapphire. Jaxon has told me a lot about you."

"Lunch sounds great," her father said quickly. "I can have my cook prepare something here for everyone."

"No," Jaxon said. "There's a restaurant in town where I'd like to take Sapphire. Then afterward, she and I can show Maverick around. I want him to see where I plan to construct the Ravnell Building."

"Wonderful! I'd love to see it myself," Bordella said.

Maverick tightened his lips, about to tell the man that no one had invited him. He kept from grinning when Jaxon said, "Maybe another time, Simon. My cousin and I want Sapphire to ourselves. He is determined to get to know her before I make any decisions about our relationship."

Maverick could see the wheels turning in Bordella's head, trying to come up with a reason for Phire not to leave with them.

"I'll grab my purse," Phire said, and quickly left the room.

When Bordella moved to follow her, Jaxon reached out and touched his hand. "Are you okay, Simon? You seem agitated."

"No, no, I'm fine. I just need to remind Sapphire about something."

Maverick could just imagine what he needed to remind Sapphire about. "I'd rather we talk, Mr. Bordella."

"About what?" he asked, looking at Maverick.

"Jaxon said something about this lucrative investment deal you told him about. I've got a few millions to spare."

As he figured it would, Maverick's statement caused a gleam to appear in the man's eyes. "That's wonderful. I have some free time now and could join you for lunch."

Jaxon laughed. "Another time. Maverick intends to be around for a few days, and I can certainly bring him back for dinner."

"What about this evening?" Bordella said excitedly.

"That sounds good," Maverick said, knowing he had no intention of coming back for dinner.

"I'm ready," Phire said, returning.

"Remember our earlier discussion, Sapphire," Bordella said as Jaxon led her from the parlor.

She slowed, gave her father a faint smile and said, "Trust me, Dad. There's no way I can forget it."

As soon as the car pulled away from the ranch house, Phire released a deep breath and then turned in her seat to glance at Maverick, who was sitting in the back. "How did you know I needed you to come for me? And how do the two of you know each other?"

"It's a long story, and we'll tell you everything once I get you as far away from here as I can," Maverick said.

"Thank you," she said, first to Maverick and then to Jaxon. Her mind was still whirling with questions. When they were on the main road that bordered her father's property, she saw four other vehicles parked there. When Jaxon pulled the car to the shoulder of the road, several men got out of the other cars.

"Who are they?" she asked Maverick, as he was getting out, too.

"Friends of Cole and Clint. All Texas Rangers. They were here in case we had trouble getting you out of there. And the other guy, the one who is taller than me and wearing a brown Stetson, is my cousin Zane Westmoreland from Denver. He came to town to pick up a horse from Clint."

"Oh," she said, studying the man he'd referred to. There was a strong resemblance between him, Clint, Cole and Maverick.

When Maverick opened the door for her, Jaxon got out and said, "I'll go let the guys know how things went back there." He then walked to where Clint and Cole were standing while talking to the group.

When Jaxon left, Phire turned to Maverick. He pulled her into his arms and captured her mouth with his. She felt desire in every stroke of his tongue and returned the kiss with just as much greed as he put into it. She honestly hadn't known he would come, but he had. Although her mind was filled with a million questions, she was satisfied with this. Being thoroughly kissed by him.

When he released her mouth, he said, "I've been worried sick since not being able to reach you last night, Phire."

"My father's housekeeper took my phone and when I tried to stop her, it landed in a bathtub filled with water." She swiped at her tears and added, "I was hoping you knew that I needed you. This was one time when I wanted you to show up and claim me and your baby. How did you know Dad was keeping me against my will?"

"Jaxon called me."

How did Jaxon know? "But how did the two of you meet?" she asked him.

"We met when Jaxon came out to Clint's ranch to see me."

"But why? How?" she asked, not understanding.

"To inform me that he's my cousin."

"Your cousin? He's a Westmoreland?"

Maverick smiled. "No, and I'll explain everything as soon as I get you settled." He brushed back a strand of hair from her face and the tears from her eyes. "My top priority is getting you as far away from here as I can."

"Where are we going?" she asked, truly not caring as long as she was with him.

"I'm flying you home."

She lifted an eyebrow. "To Paris?"

He shook his head. "No. I'm taking you to my home in Alaska."

Sixteen

As the Outlaw Freight Lines company jet cleared the Austin runway and tilted its wings toward Alaska, Maverick glanced down at the woman who slept in his arms. He was certain he'd aged ten years last night after getting that call from Jaxon letting him know Phire was being held by her father against her will. He'd almost become the outlaw Phire often teased him about being. It had taken his cousins' calm demeanor, which included Jaxon's, to keep him from storming Bordella's ranch last night.

He had called Garth, who had contacted his brothers and the other Westmorelands, and let them know what was going on. They'd sent word that they were poised and ready for action if needed. He'd even gotten a call early this morning from his Navy SEAL cousin, Bane, stating he and his team members and friends, who were home awaiting their next mission, had no problem flying to Austin to rescue Phire. They could get her out without anyone on Bordella's ranch even knowing they'd been invaded.

Maverick had appreciated everyone's support and offers of assistance, but had told them to hold tight. He figured that he, Cole, Clint, Zane and Jaxon could handle things for now. Of course, that meant explaining to everyone who Jaxon was. His brothers and the Westmorelands were looking forward to meeting him.

Although Maverick had also told Garth to hang tight, he hadn't been surprised when his oldest brother had called first thing this morning to let him know that he and his pilot wife, Regan, were on their way to get him and Phire in the company jet.

Maverick and Jaxon figured once Phire didn't return to the Bordella ranch within a reasonable time, her father would suspect something was not on the up-and-up. For that reason, Jaxon had called Bordella before takeoff and told him that his cousin Maverick had been so taken with Phire that Jaxon had impulsively asked Phire to fly to his home in Virginia to meet his other relatives. She had agreed and they were on their way now in his company's jet.

Jaxon mentioned he would take her shopping when they got to Virginia and not to expect them back for a few days. Bordella was smart enough not to push back on Jaxon's impulsive actions and risk his ire. When Bordella asked to speak to Phire, probably to remind her again of his threats, Jaxon said he would have her call him back later.

Maverick cuddled Phire in his arms. She had dozed off the moment they'd boarded, and he figured she hadn't gotten much sleep last night. When they had arrived at the airport, he had introduced Phire to Garth and Regan, and told Jaxon he would see him in a few hours. Jaxon would be trailing behind them in his own private jet to Alaska.

Maverick drew in a deep breath as he gently caressed the side of Phire's face, intending never to let her out of his sight again. He wanted her to sleep for as long as she could because he was not in any hurry to tell her the rest of what he knew, especially about her aunt.

However, the first thing he wanted to do was make sure she knew how he felt about her. They had some serious talking to do. Knowing they had several hours of flight time ahead of them, he leaned back against the seat, stretched out his legs and closed his eyes as well.

In her sleep, Phire thought she heard Maverick's husky voice repeating her name while showering kisses along her cheeks and upper lip. She didn't want to open her eyes, fearful that when she did, her dream would end. So instead, she cuddled deeper into his arms to enjoy what he was doing. And when she began getting aroused, she moaned out his name.

"Wake up, baby, the plane has landed."

His words had her opening her eyes to stare into his dark ones. "Maverick?"

"Yes?"

She reached up to touch his bearded chin. "You're really here."

"Yes, I'm really here."

She glanced around and saw they were on a plane and then she remembered and jerked up in his lap.

"Easy, or you're going to fall out of my lap."

She looked up at him. "You held me the entire trip?"

"Yes. I needed to hold you."

Leaning up, she glanced out the window. "I'm really in Alaska?"

He chuckled. "Yes, you're really in Alaska."

She looked toward the cockpit. "Where's your brother and his wife?"

"They've deplaned already and are checking in with the tower. We will see them tomorrow."

"We will?"

"Yes. My siblings and I will hold our own meeting at my place before we meet with our dad. I want you there with me so I can introduce you to him."

"Attend a meeting with your dad? But I have nothing to wear. This is all I have. I didn't pack anything, remember?"

"Yes, I remember. It's been taken care of."

Phire lifted an eyebrow. "It has?"

"Yes."

Lifting her off her lap, he said, "My brother Sloan is bringing the car to the plane since you don't have a coat. For now, here's my jacket," he said, pulling off his blazer and placing it around her shoulders.

"What about you?"

He chuckled. "I'm an Alaskan and used to the cold."

When they stepped off the jet, a sleek car pulled up and a guy who resembled Maverick was driving. She blinked, thinking he favored Clint, Cole and that other Westmoreland guy she'd been introduced to. The one named Zane. They were all extremely handsome men. "Strong Outlaw genes," she said.

"No, strong Westmoreland genes."

He introduced her to his brother Sloan, who told her that his wife, Leslie, was looking forward to meeting her. It didn't take them long to get to Maverick's home, which was located less than fifteen miles from the airport. Sloan kept things lively during the drive, telling Phire that he and his wife were expecting their first baby in June and the doctor had confirmed they were having a girl. They were ecstatic about it.

Phire was impressed with Maverick's house the minute the car pulled into the driveway of a huge modern-style split level. The yard was completely covered with snow. She'd never seen this much snow ever. "Your house is beautiful, Maverick."

"Thanks. I bought it last year. Before then, I lived in a condo in town."

Since neither of them had luggage, Maverick swept her into his arms after they'd thanked and said goodbye to Sloan, saying the ice on his walkway was slippery and he didn't want her to fall. The moment he opened the door to his home, she was in awe. It was beautiful and the decor looked amazing.

"I have my cousin Gemma to thank for this. She

lives in Australia with her husband, Callum. She did the decorating for me."

"She did an awesome job."

"I think so, too," he said, placing her on her feet. She saw the numerous shopping bags on his sofa and said, "Those are yours. I called my sister Charm, and she was more than happy to go shopping for you. I told her your size."

She glanced over at him. "And you know my size?"

He pulled her into his arms. "I believe I do."

He probably did, she thought, but she wondered if he'd taken into consideration that certain parts of her were beginning to expand. "I want to see what's all in those bags."

"Later," he said. "We need to talk."

She nodded. However, there was something she needed from him first. The moment she'd entered the parlor at her father's home and had seen him, those overactive hormones had pushed her desire buttons. She wasn't sure how long they would stay here before she returned to Paris, but it didn't matter. She intended to get in all the lovemaking she could.

"I really want to do something else first, Maverick," she said, wrapping her arms around his neck.

"And just what is it you want to do, Phire?"

"Make love with you."

His smile widened as he swept her off her feet and into his strong arms. In no time he'd made it up the stairs and placed her on the bed. Glancing around, she saw just how spacious his bedroom was and his furniture looked big and sturdy.

She was about to ask him about the various framed

artworks on the wall when he began undressing her. The moment he removed her dress and touched her breasts, any further questions evaporated from her mind. All she could concentrate on was what he was doing and how he was doing it.

"They look bigger."

She chuckled. "They are bigger."

"Will you be breastfeeding our baby?"

"Yes, I plan on it."

"Good. I'm sure, like its father, he or she will enjoy your nipples."

When he reached out and placed a hand on her stomach, the warmth of it against her skin made her moan. "If you do that in a few weeks, you'll get more than you bargained for."

He looked up at her. "What will I get?"

"Probably a kick. Our baby will start moving soon."

"I can't wait."

She rolled her eyes. "Only because you're not the one who will constantly be feeling those kicks."

"I could be feeling them if a certain part of me stayed inside of you the majority of the time."

Her pulse leaped as his words stirred a sensuous visual image in her mind. She tilted back her head to look at him. "Um…as nice as that sounds, I don't think it's possible. But for now, it is. The part about you being inside of me."

He eased away to remove his clothes and when he returned, he caressed her all over as if needing to verify the fact that she was there with him. The way he stroked her skin sent sharp sensations all through her.

"Maverick…"

"I'm here, baby, and I will always be here."

And then he straddled her and clutched her hips with his strong hands, while widening her legs with his knees. When he eased inside of her, filling her in a way that only he could, her body quivered in anticipation. When he began moving, going deep and then withdrawing in long, sinuous strokes, she couldn't stop the moans flowing from her lips or the way her nails dug deep into his shoulders. And she certainly couldn't bring an end to the way her inner muscles clenched him, increasing the pace of his thrusts.

"Phire!"

"Maverick!"

Together they were swept away in a high tide of turbulent waves. She screamed his name again when she felt his body fill hers with another hot release as they both came a second time. If she hadn't been pregnant before, she would definitely have gotten pregnant now. Their lovemaking had been so compelling, so needed and so draining.

As she closed her eyes, something he said earlier coaxed her into sweet oblivion. *I'm here, baby, and I will always be here.*

Seventeen

An hour or so later, Maverick watched as Phire came awake in his arms. She gazed at him before glancing around as if to remind herself where she was.

"Thanks, Maverick."

He knew what she was thanking him for. He leaned in and kissed her lips. "Never thank me for making love to you, Phire. The pleasure was all mine." Then with seriousness, he said, "It's time for us to talk now."

She nodded and pulled herself up in bed beside him. "Alright."

"First there's something you obviously don't know and maybe I should have told you long before now."

She pushed a lock of hair back from her face. "And what's that?"

"That I love you."

She nodded. "I know you love me, Maverick. I wouldn't be your best friend if you didn't."

He took her hand in his and met her gaze. "That's where you are wrong, Phire. I love you more than just as a friend."

She blinked. Then she blinked again, and asked, "What did you say?"

He had no problem repeating himself. "I said that I love you more than just as a friend. I love you as a man would love a woman he wanted, needed and desired. A woman he wants more than anything to spend the rest of his life with."

"Because of the baby?" she asked in a soft voice.

"No. I believe I fell in love with you a long time ago. I just wouldn't admit it to myself. Now I understand why I felt so hurt when you ended our FWB relationship."

"You felt hurt?" she asked, looking deep into his eyes, as if she couldn't believe what he'd said.

"Yes. We were doing good, enjoying a fantastic relationship, and then one day I arrived in Paris, and you announced you wanted to end things."

She nodded. "There was a reason I felt I had to do that, Maverick."

"I know. You were ready to seek a serious relationship with some other guy."

"That's the reason I told you, but it wasn't the truth."

He drew his eyebrows together. "Then why did you end things with us?"

"Because I had fallen in love with you even though I knew what we'd agreed to be from the beginning—

just friends. I decided to end things to keep my heart from getting broken."

His hold on her hands tightened, as if he thought he had to keep her captured with them. "Are you saying you love me?"

"Yes. I've always loved you, Maverick. I think I fell in love with you that night you walked into Du-Rands, although I'd convinced myself I would never love another man after what Jacques did to me. But I fell in love with you, anyway."

Maverick leaned down and brushed a kiss across her lips. "Well, I fought the idea of falling in love with you for as long as I could, but that week you spent with me at the Golden Glade made me realize what my feelings were for you. That's why I asked you to marry me. I want both you and my baby, Phire."

"I didn't know."

"Now, you do," he said, leaning toward her to capture her mouth with his. Their tongues dueled and mated, and desire stirred his insides in a way it had never done before. He always enjoyed kissing her, and realizing she loved him as much as he loved her affected him. And knowing his child grew inside of her was like the icing on the cake. But he knew there was something else she needed to know, and he needed to be the one to tell her.

He pulled back his mouth and met her gaze. "There's something else I need to tell you, Phire."

She nodded. "About how you and Jaxon are related?"

"That, too, but this is news about your aunt."

"My aunt?" she asked excitedly. "Did your cousins' security firm find her?"

"Yes."

A huge smile covered her face. "That's great! Where is she? I want to go to her, Maverick. I haven't seen her in months, and I need to see for myself that she's okay and—"

"Phire."

Evidently there was something in his tone that made her search his gaze intently. "What is it, Maverick? What's wrong?"

He tightened his hold on her hand and said, "Your aunt passed away, Phire. She died in her sleep in November."

"In November?"

"Yes. Your father ordered the facility not to inform you of your aunt's death. Instead, he called for you to come home immediately. Under the pretense that she was still alive, he hoped you'd do what he wanted you to do."

"Aunt Lois is gone?" Phire said in a soft voice as tears sprang into her eyes. "All this time Dad knew she was gone. How could he be so cruel?"

Instead of answering her, Maverick pulled her into his arms while she cried and inwardly cursed Bordella for what he'd done.

"Here, baby, drink this."

Phire took the glass of apple juice Maverick offered her. "Thanks." She didn't know how long she'd cried, but it had been until she hadn't had any tears left. And Maverick held her in his arms the entire time. He'd finally taken her out of the bedroom and brought her into the living room.

Maverick, her outlaw. The man she loved and who'd told her just an hour ago that he loved her. The news he had delivered about her aunt had been such a shock. "How could my father have lied to me about something like that?" That was the part she just couldn't get beyond.

Maverick eased down on the sofa beside her and pulled her into his arms. "I don't know, Phire. I can't imagine him lying to you that way and actually using his sister to bring you to heel."

She took a sip of her juice, then looked at him and said, "Aunt Lois wasn't his sister."

He quirked an eyebrow. "She wasn't?"

"No, she was his mother." When he eased her into his lap, she then told him what her father had shared. "She was only fourteen and he blamed her for giving him away. She was just a child, one who'd gotten raped."

"What made your father decide to hold you hostage?" Maverick asked her, gently stroking her stomach.

She frowned. "Massie found my prenatal books and told my father she suspected I was pregnant. He questioned me and I admitted I was. He said I was to seduce Jaxon into thinking he was the father or get rid of my baby. I refused to do either. That's when he had me locked in my room. What kind of father is he?"

"For one thing, he's not yours."

"What do you mean?"

While Maverick held her, he told her what Jaxon

had told them about the letter her grandfather had written to his. "Now what Dad said last night makes sense," she said softly.

"What did he say?"

"He said that I was no better than my mother." She paused. "I'm glad he's not my biological father. Now I don't have to worry about our baby one day growing up and being anything like him."

"Me, too," Maverick said, grinning. "It would have been bad enough with Bart's blood running through his veins."

She leaned up. "Now will you tell me how Jaxon knows so much and how the two of you are related?"

For the next half hour, he held her while telling her everything, including why her father was desperate for her to marry Jaxon.

"Wow, that's a lot to take in," she said, appreciating him holding her the entire time. "Just think what would have happened if Jaxon's grandfather hadn't shared all those documents with him and he hadn't had a mind to set a wrong right."

"Yes, and I can't wait for my brothers and sister to meet him. You said in the beginning that there was something about Jaxon that made you think he was playing your Dad. Now we know that was the truth." Maverick eased her from his lap and stood. "There is something else that needs to be done to make this day complete."

She looked up at him. "What?"

"This." He then eased down on bended knees before her and took her hand in his. "I asked you before and you thought it was for the wrong reason. Now I'm asking you again, and I hope you know it's for the right reason. I love you, Phire. Will you marry me?"

Tears sprang into her eyes. "Yes! I will marry you."

He slid a ring on her finger, and the huge diamond nearly blinded her. "Wow! It's beautiful, Maverick. I love it!"

"I'm glad, sweetheart. The day after you left the Golden Glade, I took Alyssa and Patrina shopping to help me pick it out. I had every intention of asking you to marry me a second time and making sure you knew how I felt about you. I love you."

"And I love you."

"Time to celebrate the Maverick Outlaw way." Standing, he swooped her off the sofa into his arms and headed for the bedroom.

The next day, Maverick and Phire got visitors—all his brothers and their wives. She also got to meet his sister Charm and thank her for shopping for her. She liked Charm immediately, as well as Maverick's four sisters-in-law.

Everyone congratulated them on their engagement and the women told Phire how much they loved her engagement ring. It was decided that she and Maverick would get married before returning to Texas and have a reception a few weeks later.

She was surprised when Jaxon arrived. Maverick said the brothers had wanted to get to know him and hear everything he had to say. Most of which she knew Maverick had heard, but he listened again along with everyone else. Garth asked a lot of questions and Jaxon had copies of all the documents that were needed. At one point they'd placed a phone call to a man named Rico Claiborne, who was married to Zane's sister, Megan. Mr. Claiborne had been the private investigator hired by the Westmorelands to find more family members connected by way of Raphel Westmoreland.

After being placed on speakerphone, Rico told them how the trail went cold after he'd traced Jeannette Outlaw to Detroit. He'd discovered she had named the child Levy, after her deceased husband.

The mother and son remained in Detroit until Levy turned twenty-one and married. He and his wife had a son they named Javier—that was who they believed Bart to be. Their grandfather Levy had changed all their first names and fled to Alaska after discovering someone was looking for him.

It amazed Phire how well the brothers and their wives got along and how easily Jaxon was included as a family member. But then, she had to admit, they were very kind to her as well and everyone had easily accepted her as the woman Maverick loved and planned to marry. Everyone knew about her pregnancy and said they were happy for them.

"I hope you understand why I couldn't tell you anything about my purpose in Texas, Phire," Jaxon said after the meeting was over. She had prepared a number of French pastries that everyone enjoyed.

She smiled up at him. "I understand, especially when you thought I was a willing accomplice in my father's scheme. And just to think, you and the Outlaws are cousins. With all the information both you and Rico provided tonight, I wonder what happens next."

"Only the Outlaws can answer that. They're calling a meeting with their father tomorrow and asked me to attend."

Phire nodded. Maverick wanted her at the meeting, too. "Tomorrow's meeting should be interesting."

Eighteen

Bart entered the conference room and glanced around, seeing his sons, his daughter and his married sons' wives. Maverick observed that his father then saw two people he didn't know. Namely, Phire and Jaxon. "What's this meeting about and who the hell are those two?" he asked gruffly.

"Let's just take a seat, Bart. I'm sure you'll meet them soon enough," Claudia said in a soothing voice, as she entered the room with him. She sat down and he sat in the chair beside her.

Maverick glanced over at his brothers. They hadn't known if Bart would invite Claudia to the meeting, but he was glad that she was here. Claudia knew just how to handle Bartram Outlaw when he got too overbearing.

"Now that you're here, Dad, we'll get started," Garth said. "And to answer your earlier question, introductions are in order, and I'll let Maverick do the honors."

Everyone's attention shifted to Maverick. Before standing, he smiled at Phire, who was seated beside him. "Dad and Claudia, I'd like you to meet Sapphire Bordella, better known as Phire. She is the woman I love and plan to marry as soon as it can be arranged."

"Marry!" Bart exclaimed, his stare moving from Maverick to Phire.

"Yes, marry," Maverick said, glaring at his father. "Do you have a problem with it, Dad?" Everyone knew that of all Bart's sons, Maverick might be the most fun-loving, but he would be the one least tolerant of Bart's interference in his life.

Bart and Maverick's eyes held and then Bart said, "No, I don't have a problem with it. In fact, I want to congratulate the two of you."

Maverick fought back a smile and figured Claudia had given their father a hard kick under the table. "Thanks, Dad." It didn't surprise Maverick when Claudia got up from the table and came around to give Phire a huge hug.

When Claudia settled back in her seat, Maverick then introduced Jaxon, saying only that he was a family friend.

"Now, I turn the meeting back over to Garth," Maverick said, sitting back down, and then brushing a kiss across Phire's lips.

Garth stood. "The reason for today's meeting,

Dad, is that we think the time has come for you to face some real important facts."

Bart frowned at his oldest son. "What facts are you talking about?"

"That we have Westmoreland blood running through our veins."

The room got quiet and when Bart didn't stand to make a scene or storm out of the room, Garth continued. "Now more than any other time we need to know the truth, whatever it is, and accept it."

"Why?" Bart snapped.

"Because millions could be at stake," Garth said. The Outlaw brothers knew the mention of money would interest Bart.

"How so?" Bart asked.

"This is where we will let Jaxon explain," Garth said, then took his seat.

Jaxon stood. "Mr. Outlaw, I have reason to believe you're the Riggins heir."

Bart rolled his eyes. "First Westmorelands, and now someone by the name of Riggins wants to claim the Outlaws?" he said in a snort.

A smile touched Jaxon's lips. "I guess you can say that since your father was conceived by Raphel Westmoreland and Clarice Riggins."

When Bart opened his mouth to deny such a thing, Jaxon held up a hand to stop him. "Please let me present my proof before you state your denials, Mr. Outlaw."

Maverick and his brothers had fully expected their father to tell Jaxon just what he could do with his proof. When Bart glanced over at Claudia, Maverick wasn't sure just what unspoken communication passed between the two. But maybe it had been a warning from Claudia. All they knew was that after breaking eye contact with Claudia, Bart glanced back at Jaxon, nodded and then said in a brusque tone, "Okay, state your case."

Like an attorney in a courtroom representing Raphel and Clarice in a child-custody suit, Jaxon presented his case. Although nobody said a word, all eyes were on Bart. Their father wore his poker face, which meant none of them had a clue what he was thinking.

Jaxon was good and there was no doubt in Maverick's mind the man had a law degree. The legal documents he had presented could not be denied. He effectively explained why Levy, his wife and their child fled from Detroit and changed their first names. Levy became Noah, his wife Elouise became Abigail and their son's name—Javier—was changed to Bartram. Upon arriving on Kodiak Island, Alaska, with little money, they were befriended by Walker and Lora Rafferty—Garth's best friend's grandparents. They had given them a place to stay and food to eat. In fact, it was the elder Raffertys who'd sold Bart's parents land to build their first home. The cabin on Kodiak Island that the Outlaws still owned.

A half hour later, Jaxon was still presenting documentation to substantiate everything he was saying. There was no doubt in anyone's mind that he was presenting a compelling case.

"I've heard enough!" Bart suddenly said, slamming his fist on the table. He stood and left the room.

Claudia stood, looked around at everyone and smiled. "I suggest we take a fifteen-minute break. I'll make sure Bart comes back."

True to her word, fifteen minutes later Bart and Claudia entered the room. After closing the door behind them, Claudia said, "Before you continue, Jaxon, Bart has something he needs to say."

Claudia sat down and the room was quiet, waiting for Bart to speak. For once he was not wearing a poker face. Anguish was etched in his eyes and his sons and daughter saw it.

Shoving his hands into his pockets, he looked at Jaxon. "I need to speak with my sons and my daughter privately."

Jaxon nodded and moved toward the door. When Phire, Regan and the other wives stood to leave, Garth said in a firm voice, "Our wives and fiancée stay. They are part of this family."

Bart opened his mouth to say something, then as if he thought better of doing so, he nodded "Yes, of course." He hesitated and then said, "For the past two months I've been seeing a therapist in New York."

Maverick was certain that although no one made a sound, just like him, his brothers were picking their jaws up off the floor.

"Something I saw at your wedding, Jess, left me totally shaken," Bart added.

"And what did you see, Dad?" Jess asked.

"It was a framed portrait inside that building where your reception was held. I had Claudia ask someone about it and they told her it was a picture of Stern Westmoreland, Raphel Westmoreland's son."

"What about the portrait?" Cash asked.

Bart didn't say anything for a long moment. "It was just like seeing my daddy. They were almost identical, right down to the mole above the lip. I couldn't believe it."

He paused again. "I'm not obtuse. I've seen the similarities between my sons and those Westmorelands, but I still refused to consider it could be true until I saw that portrait."

"Why did you get this sudden epiphany when you saw that picture, Dad?" Maverick asked. He wondered how his father would handle it when it was disclosed that Stern Westmoreland was Bart's father's half brother since they'd shared the same father, Raphel Westmoreland. That was the reason the two men looked so much alike. Those strong Westmoreland genes.

"Not only were his features almost identical to those of my father, but his eyes—it was like staring at my Dad. Like I said, seeing it shook me up real bad."

Everyone got quiet and then Sloan asked, "Dad, do you recall ever being called *Javier*?"

"No. And I've never known my father to be called *Levy*, either. He was Noah. And my birth certificate says I was born here, in Alaska, to Noah and Abigail Outlaw. But the one thing I do recall as a child is Dad buying that land from Walker's grandfather and the two of them building that cabin."

"Do you know why there's an underground tunnel and why Granddad had all those guns?" Maverick asked his father.

"Yes," Bart said. "He told me there were people who were part of some group, sort of like a cult, that wanted to change our identity and that if they ever showed up in Alaska looking for us that he would be ready."

Bart paused and then added, "While growing up, both my father and mother would tell me to protect the Outlaw name because we were Outlaws, and not to believe it if someone ever tried to tell me differently. Dad stressed the same thing to me on his deathbed and made me promise I would protect the Outlaw name."

The room got quiet again. Now Maverick understood and knew his siblings did as well. Jeannette Outlaw had pretty much brainwashed her son, Levy, into believing he was the biological son of her deceased husband, Levy Outlaw, Sr., for fear he would be taken away from her. It sounded like she concocted this big lie about a cult. No wonder the man had fled from the lower forty-eight to Alaska, believing he was protecting his family.

"After listening to Jaxon, you do see there's a possibility what he's saying is true, Dad, right?" Charm asked. "He has the documentation to prove it."

Bart glanced over at his only daughter and his face softened. "I don't want to see it because that would mean my father lied to me, Charm, and my father would never have lied to me."

"He probably told you what he believed was the truth," Maverick said. "His adoptive mother felt she had reason to keep him away from the biological grandfather looking for him, the man who wanted to take him away from her. That's why she lied. Her son was all she had."

Maverick wondered if his father recalled that he'd acted that same way when the Westmorelands first reached out to them. They'd been grown men, yet Bart had acted as if they were children and had forbidden them to have a relationship with the Westmorelands. And he'd honestly expected his directive to be followed.

"I promised Dad on his deathbed that I would uphold the Outlaw name and its legacy," Bart said. Everyone could hear the pain in his voice.

"Just because we have Westmoreland and Riggins blood running through our veins doesn't mean we aren't Outlaws, Dad," Garth said. "We *are* Outlaws. Nothing will ever change that."

"Garth is right, Dad," Jess said. "We are Outlaws and there's nothing wrong in discovering we're related to others. After meeting Jaxon, we're claiming him as kin the same way we do the Westmorelands."

The room got quiet and then Maverick said, "We would like you to hear the rest of what Jaxon has to say. Tillman Riggins never gave up looking for your father. He even put a clause in his will for the search to continue after his death. He left money for that to happen. Money that Phire's father has misused over the years."

Bart raised an eyebrow as he glanced across the table at Phire. "Your father?"

"My stepfather," she corrected.

"In order for you to stop Simon Bordella and claim what was rightfully Granddad's, and now yours," Sloan said, "you have to admit you are the Riggins heir."

"Well, what do you think your father will do?" Phire asked Maverick when they returned to his house later that day. Jaxon had returned to the meeting and Bart had listened to what he had to say without interrupting.

"Jaxon certainly did a great job explaining everything and he had all the legal documents to prove it," Maverick said, closing the door behind them. "I talked to my siblings after the meeting. We knew there was a reason Dad refused to accept the Westmorelands. Now we see it was more than him being ornery and pigheaded."

"Well, I think it's admirable that he decided to seek help with a therapist."

"Don't get it twisted, Phire. I'll bet a million dollars seeing a therapist wasn't Dad's idea, but Claudia's."

Phire dropped down on the sofa to remove her boots. "Is there really a cabin with an escape tunnel and an arsenal of weapons?"

Maverick came to sit down beside her, reached over and placed her legs in his lap to remove her boots for her. "Yes. My siblings and I never knew the reason for the secret passageway or why an arsenal of guns was kept there. Now the mystery has been solved."

Maverick dropped her boots to the floor. "Are you ready to marry an outlaw?"

Phire couldn't help the smile that spread across her face. "Yes. When?"

He smiled. "Is tomorrow soon enough? Since there's a three-day wait in Alaska, let's fly to Canada tomorrow to get married."

"That sounds good to me," Phire said, wrapping her arms around his neck. "Jaxon said Dad keeps calling, wanting to talk to me. That's what he gets for trying to take my phone. Since it's damaged, he can't reach me."

"Jaxon did mention your father keeps calling him. He told Bordella that you're extending your stay until this weekend. That will give us time to get married and wait for Bart to decide what he will do."

"I guess Dad's hoping I'll use that time to seduce Jaxon so he'll think my baby is his." Phire didn't say anything for a long moment. "What happens if your father doesn't admit to being the Riggins heir? Will Dad get to keep the ranch and land?"

"Not if me and my siblings can help it. It would be less messy and an easier process in court if Bart cooperated. However, if he doesn't, my siblings and I can certainly prove we're descendants of Levy Outlaw. We've decided that with or without Bart, we're going to handle your father. There's no way I'm going to let him get away with what he did, especially to you."

"I now pronounce you husband and wife. Maverick Outlaw, you may kiss your bride."

Maverick pulled Phire into his arms and captured her lips. He'd figured it would be just the two of them with Garth and Regan as witnesses. But when they'd landed in Vancouver, the rest of the Outlaw brothers and their wives, along with Charm and Jaxon, were waiting on them.

When he released Phire's mouth, he whispered, "I love you, Mrs. Outlaw."

She smiled up at him. "And I love you, Maverick, my outlaw."

After the ceremony, everyone joined them for dinner at a restaurant not far from the chapel where they'd gotten married. The food was great, and Maverick wanted to pinch himself knowing he had married his best friend and they were having a baby.

Garth excused himself from the table when his cell phone rang. Maverick figured it was some kind of business call. When Garth returned moments later, he said, "Well, I'll be damned." Everyone looked over at Garth when he sat back down at the table with his phone still in his hand.

"What?" Maverick asked.

"That was Bart, and he intends to go to Texas to claim what's his."

Nineteen

Simon glanced up when there was a knock on his office door. "What is it?"

Massie opened the door and stepped inside. "Your daughter has returned."

"About time," he said, standing. "Is Jaxon with her?"

"Yes, along with several others, including that man who came with him the last time."

Simon nodded. "Where are they?"

"I've seated everyone in the parlor. There's something else you should know."

"What?"

"Your daughter is wearing a wedding ring. A very expensive-looking one."

A huge smile touched Simon's face. He'd known

when Jaxon had whisked Sapphire off to Virginia that there had to have been a plan behind it. For a while, he'd been worried that Sapphire wouldn't do as she was told, but things had worked out just the way he'd wanted. "Those other people with Jaxon are probably other family members. Tell Cal to bring out the best wine and whiskey. This calls for a celebration."

When Massie closed the door, Simon came from around his desk and leaned against it. With Sapphire married it should be easy enough to persuade Jaxon to buy all that land. Like he'd told his servant, today was one to celebrate.

Drawing in a deep, satisfied breath, he left his office and headed toward the parlor.

"Remember, Dad, let Jaxon do the talking," Maverick told Bart, who merely grunted a response.

All Maverick's brothers were there. Also present were Clint, Cole and Zane. Zane was supposed to have left to return home days ago, but said there was no way he would return to Denver with all the action about to go down.

Also present was Jaxon's attorney, along with the Outlaws' attorney. Based on the proof Jaxon had in his possession, both attorneys had worked together for the last two days to obtain proper documentation certifying Bart as the rightful descendant of the Riggins heir.

For once, Bart hadn't questioned the Westmorelands' presence. Maverick and his brothers figured it was because of the test results that had come back yesterday that showed Bart's DNA was a match for both Raphel and Clarice. They were able to get Raphel's DNA verification by way of the Zane Wesmoreland. He'd been more than happy to assist.

Such a revelation had to have had a jarring effect on Bart. They were glad Claudia was there to give him whatever support he needed. Hopefully, those therapy sessions would help him come to terms with his true family history.

"Jaxon and Sapphire, you have returned."

Everyone's attention was drawn to the man who'd entered the parlor. Simon smiled at everyone, and then his gaze went back to Jaxon. "I assume these people are your family."

"Yes, they are," Jaxon said, smiling, and then he began making introductions.

"I understand you and Sapphire have news for me," Simon said. It hadn't gone unnoticed by everyone that other than acknowledging Phire when he'd entered the room, he hadn't approached her with a hug.

"And what kind of news do you think we have for you, Dad?" Phire asked, smiling. Maverick wondered if her father found it odd that she was standing beside him and not Jaxon.

"I'd think that wedding ring on your finger says it all, Sapphire."

"Not quite, Simon," Jaxon said with a smile that didn't quite reach his eyes. "What I didn't mention during the introductions was that Mr. Barnett is my attorney and Mr. Coker is the Outlaws'."

Simon's eyebrows drew together. "Attorneys?

Surely you're not going to tell me any nonsense about a prenuptial agreement."

Jaxon chuckled. "Of course, I wouldn't tell you any such nonsense. However, I am telling you that you have twenty-four hours to vacate these premises, leaving everything as it is and making sure you take all your servants with you."

A deep frown settled on Simon's face. "What the hell are you talking about?"

"Just what I said. We have proof that for the past twenty-five years you have been living on property that doesn't belong to you," Jaxon stated.

"That's a lie. If this ranch doesn't belong to me then who in the hell does it belong to?"

Before Jaxon could answer, Bart came forward and in Bart Outlaw fashion got in Simon's face. "It belongs to me, so get your thieving ass off my land."

Simon stared at Bart. "And who the hell are you supposed to be?"

"Bart Outlaw." He hesitated for just a second, then added, "My father was the Riggins heir. Anything that was to have gone to him, I'm here to claim today."

And while her father was too shocked to speak, Phire said, "I know about Aunt Lois. You had me thinking she was still alive to try and get me to do whatever you wanted. And just so you know, I didn't marry Jaxon. I married Maverick Outlaw, the father of my baby."

"And you're sure you're okay, baby?" Maverick asked Phire, slowly breaking off their kiss. They had checked into a hotel in downtown Austin, while other members of the family joined Clint at the Golden Glade. Bart and Claudia had left to return to Alaska and the attorneys remained behind to file more paperwork with the courts.

"I'm fine. Sorry if I shocked your dad when I announced my pregnancy."

"Don't worry about Bart. He loves seeing the Outlaw family increasing."

"That's good to hear, and I tried to warn you that Dad wouldn't leave willingly."

Yes, she had, and he was glad Clint had the Texas Rangers on stand-by to escort Simon off the premises. They would join the family at Clint's ranch tomorrow for lunch. Then his brothers and their wives, along with Jaxon and Charm, would fly with them to Paris. Everyone understood Phire's need to give her aunt a proper memorial service.

Regardless of whether the woman had been her aunt or her grandmother, Phire loved her and appreciated her giving her the love she had needed after losing her mother.

"Well, Simon Bordella's insolence got him arrested," Maverick said, pulling her into his arms and smoothing his hand down her back, then lower to her backside. When he shifted his stance, he knew she felt the hardness of his erection poking into her middle. "And Bart doesn't intend to let him get away with anything. He'll have to make restitution for any funds he used illegally."

"Serves him right. While listening to Jaxon state all my stepfather had done, it made me glad he wasn't my biological father. It also made me appreciate my grandfather for being Tillman Riggins's trusted attorney and for him having the hindsight to send all those documents to Jaxon's grandfather."

"Me, too. Without Jaxon's intervention, and letting the Outlaws know what was going on, your father would have gotten away with it," Maverick said, sweeping Phire off her feet.

He was glad his father had had the decency to thank Jaxon, and it had made his brothers feel good when he had welcomed the man to the family. They'd warned Jaxon not to get too giddy about it, since it might end up being a curse more than a blessing. You never knew with Bart.

He placed Phire on the bed. "You think my son or daughter is ready for another visit from their old man?" he said, unbuttoning his shirt.

"They would welcome your visit at any time. It was kind of the Outlaw ladies to help me plan our wedding reception. They know we can't put it off too much longer if I want to fit into a nice gown."

The reception would be held on Cash's ranch in Wyoming since February wasn't the best time for anyone to travel to Alaska. After he completely undressed himself, he then reached out for his wife. She had been this Outlaw's claim, and he would never regret making it.

Epilogue

Phire glanced up at the man who was holding her in his arms while they shared a dance. He was not only her best friend and husband, but he was also her everything. "Thanks for making arrangements to have Clancy and his family and the DuRands fly here. That meant a lot to me."

Maverick smiled down at her. "I figured it would. I told him of my plans when we flew to Paris for your aunt's memorial service. I also told him not to tell you because it was a secret."

"And it was a wonderful one."

"And you're okay with us living in Alaska and not Paris?" he asked, holding her close.

"Yes, but then there's no other place I'd rather be than where you are. Sloan's wife, Leslie, has given me the name of her doctor and I plan to call him when we get back from our honeymoon." Before leaving Texas, Phire had kept the appointment with her doctor. The look on Maverick's face when he'd heard their child's heartbeat had been priceless.

She paused and then said, "It was kind of your father to give us the ranch and the land it sits on as a wedding gift."

Maverik nodded. "Yes, it was, but then look at how much land he kept. Over two thousand acres. I have a feeling he'll be giving each of my other brothers and Charm acres of their own as well. Even after that, Dad will still have plenty land left for himself."

Phire glanced across the room to where Bart and Claudia were talking to Dillon and his wife, Pam. At least Claudia was doing the talking—Bart was just listening. Maverick had said his father wasn't all that sociable and finding out about his family history hadn't changed that about him. "Do you think your father and Claudia will eventually get married?"

Maverick followed her gaze. "Yes, one day. There's no way Dad will let her get away a second time. Enough about everyone else—let's talk about us. Are you ready for our honeymoon?"

They would be flying out tomorrow for Jamaica. He said he wanted to take her someplace where there was a lot of sunlight since when they returned to Alaska, the days would be short and cold. "Yes, I'm definitely ready. I even got a bathing suit. I figured I better wear it now while I can still look sexy."

When the music came to an end, he pulled her

closer. "Baby, you'll look sexy even if it's the day before you deliver our baby." He then lowered his head to hers for a kiss.

Jaxon took a sip of his champagne while watching the woman across the room talking with Zane. He had met most of the members of the Westmoreland family and wondered who she was. He thought she was beautiful, or *striking* was a more appropriate word.

"You're enjoying yourself, Jaxon?"

He nodded to Jess. "I'm fine. There are a lot of Westmorelands."

Jess chuckled. "Yes, there are. Now you can imagine how my brothers and I felt meeting them for the first time. They are a right friendly group who are big on family. I understand Dillon welcomed you to the Westmoreland family and introduced you to the Atlanta and Montana Westmorelands."

"He did, but he really didn't have to do that since I'm not related to them," Jaxon said, taking another sip of his champagne.

"You're related to us, which makes you related to them. That's the Westmoreland way."

"And what about that woman standing over there talking to Zane? Is she a member of the family?"

Jess followed his gaze. "That's Nadia Novak and, yes, we consider her a member of the family." He then studied Jaxon and said, "But not to the point where you can't approach her if you're interested."

Jaxon switched his gaze from Nadia back to Jess.

"You sure? You did say she was considered part of the Westmoreland family."

"Yes, I'm sure. I can say that with certainty since my wife, Paige, is Nadia's sister. And so is Aidan's wife, Jillian, and Dillon's wife, Pam. Three out of four sisters married Westmoreland men."

A smile spread across Jaxon's face. "You don't say?"

"I do say. However, I'll give you fair warning—Nadia is as feisty as they come."

Jaxon chuckled. "I love feistiness in a woman."

Jess threw back his head and laughed. "Then you'll definitely love Nadia. Come on and let me introduce the two of you."

Jaxon followed Jess across the room. He had a feeling that after meeting Nadia Novak, his life would never be the same again.

"All your sons are now married, Bart, to strong women. You have to feel good about that."

He looked over at Claudia. "I am. They are married and producing more Outlaws."

"Now all that's left is Charm to marry."

Bart snorted. "I'm not ready for that."

"Well, you need to get ready. She'll be thirty in a couple of years."

Bart frowned. "And?"

"And I think it's time you tell her what you did all those years ago. It's best she hears it from you and not find out on her own."

"I did the right thing, Claudia. She was too young to think herself in love. It was utter teenage nonsense."

"She might not agree with you about that, especially when she discovers what you did to break up her and Dylan Emanuel."

Bart didn't say anything for a moment. "I might lose her if I told her."

"And you might lose her if you don't tell her."

Bart glanced across the room, to where Charm was talking to Cash and his wife Brianna. Charm was his pride and joy and the thought of losing his only daughter was a pain he couldn't endure.

He'd done what he thought was best, and he'd leave it at that.

* * * * *

Don't miss a single installment of
Westmoreland Legacy: The Outlaws
from USA TODAY *bestselling author*
Brenda Jackson

The Wife He Needs
The Marriage He Demands
What He Wants for Christmas
What Happens on Vacation…
The Outlaw's Claim

And Charm's story, coming summer 2023!

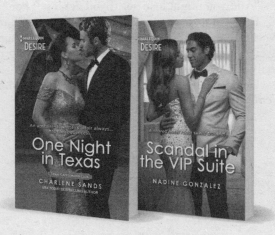

COMING NEXT MONTH FROM

DESIRE

#2911 ONE CHRISTMAS NIGHT

Texas Cattleman's Club: Ranchers and Rivals
by Jules Bennett

Ryan Carter and Morgan Grandin usually fight like cats and dogs—until one fateful night at a Texas Cattleman's Club masquerade ball. Now will an unexpected pregnancy make these hot-and-heavy enemies permanent lovers?

#2912 MOST ELIGIBLE COWBOY

Devil's Bluffs • by Stacey Kennedy

Brokenhearted journalist Adeline Harlow is supposed to write an exposé on Colter Ward, Texas's Sexiest Bachelor, *not* fall into bed with him enthusiastically and repeatedly! If only it's enough to break their no-love-allowed rule for a second chance at happiness...

#2913 A VALENTINE FOR CHRISTMAS

Valentine Vineyards • by Reese Ryan

Prodigal son Julian Brandon begrudgingly returns home to fulfill a promise. Making peace with his troubled past and falling for sophisticated older woman Chandra Valentine aren't part of the plan. But what is it they say about best-laid plans...?

#2914 WORK-LOVE BALANCE

Blackwells of New York • by Nicki Night

When gorgeous TV producer Jordan Chambers offers Ivy Blackwell the chance of a lifetime, the celebrated heiress and social media influencer wonders if she can handle his tempting offer...and the passion that sizzles between them!

#2915 TWO RIVALS, ONE BED

The Eddington Heirs • by Zuri Day

Stakes can't get much higher for attorneys Maeve Eddington and Victor Cortez in the courtroom...or in the bedroom. With family fortunes on the line, these rivals will go to any lengths to win. But what if love is the ultimate prize?

#2916 BILLIONAIRE MAKEOVER

The Image Project • by Katherine Garbera

When PR whiz Olive Hayes transforms scruff CEO Dante Russo into the industry's sexiest bachelor, she realizes she's equally vulnerable to his charms. But is she falling for her new creation or the man underneath the makeover?

SPECIAL EXCERPT FROM

HARLEQUIN

DESIRE

Thanks to violinist Megan Han's one-night fling with her father's new CFO, Daniel Pak, she's pregnant! No one can know the truth—especially not her matchmaking dad, who'd demand marriage. If only her commitment-phobic not-so-ex lover would open his heart…

Read on for a sneak peek at
One Night Only
by Jayci Lee.

The sway of Megan's hips mesmerized him as she glided down the walkway ahead of him. He caught up with her in three long strides and placed his hand on her lower back. His nostrils flared as he caught a whiff of her sweet floral scent, and reason slipped out of his mind.

He had been determined to keep his distance since the night she came over to his place. He didn't want to betray Mr. Han's trust further. And it wouldn't be easy for Megan to keep another secret from her father. The last thing he wanted was to add to her already full plate. But when he saw her standing in the garden tonight—a vision in her flowing red dress—he knew he would crawl through burning coal to have her again.

She reached for his hand, and he threaded his fingers through hers, and she pulled them into a shadowy alcove and pressed her back against the wall. He placed his hands on either side of her head and stared at her face until his eyes adjusted to the dark. He sucked in a sharp breath when she slid her palms over his chest and wrapped her arms around his neck.

"I don't want to burden you with another secret to keep from your father." He held himself in check even as desire pumped through his veins.

"I think fighting this attraction between us is the bigger burden," she whispered. His head dipped toward her of its own volition, and she wet her lips. "What are you doing, Daniel?"

"Surviving," he said, his voice a low growl. "Because I can't live through another night without having you."

She smiled then—a sensual, triumphant smile—and he was lost.

Don't miss what happens next in...
One Night Only
by Jayci Lee.

Available December 2022 wherever Harlequin Desire books and ebooks are sold.

Harlequin.com

HDEXP1022